HOW TO ENSNARE THE PERFECT DUKE

(WAYWARD DUKES' ALLIANCE - BOOK 5)

TABETHA WAITE

Copyright © 2023 Tabetha Waite

Cover Design by Mandy Koehler Designs

This title is a work of fiction. Names, characters, places, brands, media, and incidents are either the product of the author's imagination or are used fictitiously. Any resemblance to similarly named places or to persons living or deceased is purely coincidental.

All rights reserved. This book or any portion thereof may not be reproduced or used in any manner whatsoever, including but not limited to photocopy, digital, auditory, and/or in print, without the express written permission of the author except for the use of brief quotations for a review.

ALSO BY TABETHA WAITE

Also by Tabetha Waite

Ways of Love Historical Romance Series

How it All Began for the Baron (0.5 prequel novella)

Why the Earl is After the Girl (Book 1)

Where the Viscount Met His Match (Book 2)

When a Duke Pursues a Lady (Book 3)

Who the Marquess Dares to Desire (Book 4)

What a Gentleman Does for Love (Book 5)

Season of the Spinster Series

Triana's Spring Seduction (Book 1)

Isabella's Secret Summer (Book 2)

The Spinster's Alluring Season (Book 2.5 novella)

Alyssa's Autumn Affair (Book 3)

Korina's Wild Winter (Book 4)

Wanton Wastrels

The Rapscallion's Romance

The Marauder's Mistress

Sensual Scandals

A Jolly Little Scandal (0.5 novella)

An Innocent Little Scandal (Book 1)

A Promising Little Scandal (Book 2)

A Dangerous Little Scandal (Book 3)

Novellas

The Harlot's Hero

Frozen Fancy

The Piper's Paramour

His Yuletide Dove

How to Choose the Perfect Scoundrel

How to Ensnare the Perfect Duke

Novels

Behind a Moonlit Veil

The Secrets of Shadows

The Visions From Dreams

Kiernan Fantasy Series

The Kingdoms of Kiernan (Kiernan – Book 1)

The Hour of Kiernan (Kiernan – Book 2)

Shared Worlds

Vanquished (K Bromberg's Driven World)

Collections

An Everlasting Christmas Amour

A Promise Beneath the Kissing Bough

Twelve Gifts by Christmas

Miss Pageant's Christmas Proposal

An Everlasting Regency Amour

The Scot's Bairn

A Lady's Guide to Marriage

Lord Castleford's Fortunate Folly

With BONUS short story – Four Calling Cards

An Everlasting Regency Amour – Volume 2

A TALE OF TWO BRUNETTES

The Brunette Who Stole His Heart

In Love with a Charming Brunette

Bedeviling Lord Coxford

A Captivating Compromise

An Everlasting Amour (A collection of various short stories)

Lords & Lace – How to Love the Perfect Lord

The Regency Abduction Club – His Sultry Captor

Christmas in Cumbria – Enchanting by Candlelight

Heyer Society (non-fiction essays)

The Garden Wedding (children's book for charity)

To those who might not have gotten together under the best circumstances, but it worked anyway.

CHAPTER 1

Summer 1816

The alliance had saved Cortland Beaumont, the Duke of Argyle, more than once. Without the assistance of his fellow Wayward Dukes, he would have had to deal with a nasty scandal, lost terribly at the gaming tables when he was in his cups, or worst yet, been married several times over. But with the help of the special signet ring on his dressing table to proclaim that he was in dire need, he had escaped any unsavory situation thus far.

Marriage was definitely on his not-to-do list. It didn't matter if he was two and thirty and his mother thought he should grant some lucky chit the honor of being a duchess. It was because of the dowager that he eschewed the wedded state of "bliss." She'd had more liaisons than he'd ever had and flaunted her latest lover in front of his father's nose. All of London knew about her peccadillos, and yet, she hadn't batted an eye at the scandals she'd caused.

Cortland could only thank God that he'd been an only child

with such an unhappy childhood. For anyone lesser, it might have caused them to end up in Bedlam. For Cortland, it just caused him to swear off matrimony for the remainder of his days.

At least he had been able to get his revenge against his mother, because as soon as his father was laid to rest, she assumed she would live life in perfect harmony with him at the estate, or at the very least, the dower house. Instead, he'd shipped her off to Scotland, to the most remote place that he could think of. He'd effectively washed his hands of her, other than the money he sent to her every month, but even his solicitors took care of that little bother. Otherwise, he didn't write, didn't visit, and frankly, he didn't care if he laid eyes on her again.

He seldom traveled to his estate and went about his daily life in London with a calm conscience.

However, he was starting to become a bit restless. In between mistresses at the moment, he decided that perhaps it was time to retire to the country for a reprieve. It was the time of season that most of his peers did the same, and he could do with a bit of hunting. Or archery, or some such outdoor sport that proclaimed him just like anyone else.

He might host a scandalous house party.

His grin widened as he sat in his study. Leaning back in the leather chair, he propped his booted feet on the top of the desk simply because there wasn't anyone there to tell him not to. He enjoyed being the ruler of his own personal kingdom, and he supposed if he wanted to throw a perfectly wicked party that involved sex, brandy, and illicit entertainment, it was his choice.

He imagined all the fun he would have and decided it was something that most definitely, needed to happen. He withdrew a sheet of paper and started to make a list of names that he would invite. All of the Wayward Dukes were invited, of course, including the honorary founder, the Duke of Cranbrook. Although Cortland didn't imagine the curmudgeonly man might actually appear, he wanted to make sure he wasn't excluded. The next time Cortland needed to call upon one of his fellow dukes, he wanted to make sure that there was someone to come to his aid.

He smiled as he started to come up with other ideas regarding the torrid gathering. He really needed to give it some sort of terribly awful title.

It would surely ensure that the manor was filled to capacity.

※

"WHAT'S THAT YOU HAVE THERE?"

The older man gave a gruff reply and quickly shoved the missive into the chair cushion. "Er... nothing. Just something idiotic."

"Indeed?" Lady Genevieve St. Giles lifted a curious eyebrow as she sat across from her grandfather and picked up that day's paper. "Sounds terribly mysterious."

"It's not, I assure you," was the firm reply.

She shrugged. "If you say so." She flipped through the pages of the black and white print and found that most of it was the same boring articles she usually perused. The same people were causing scandals. The same London fashions that she'd seen for the past few years. She yearned for a change in... *something*, no matter what it entailed. And yet, ever since the war with France had ended, it seemed as though her fellow Brits were content to remain perfectly... boring.

She wasn't upset that the war had ended, of course. On the contrary, she had enjoyed seeing families reunited, and hearing their stories of survival or even loss. At least there was some sort of emotion being shared, rather than... nothing.

Genevieve knew she sounded selfish and spoiled, but after staying at her parents' estate for the past few years, without any sort of social life, and fearing a retaliation from Napoleon's army might break through their defenses, she was ready to live. And for some reason, she kept staring at the square bit of vellum that taunted her from her grandfather's chair. With any luck, he would forget it was there and she could get her eager hands on it.

Until then, she had to make polite conversation. Perhaps his wife would return and distract him so that he would decide to rush off to his club in an effort to escape her. In Genevieve's observation, it wasn't that they despised each other. It was just what people did who had been married a long time.

As if providence answered her call, the front door opened and closed and Genevieve could hear the determined footfalls of her grandmother, the Duchess of Cranbrook, Eleanor St. Giles, crossing the marble foyer in the Mayfair townhouse.

She tried to hide a smile as her grandfather grumbled something beneath his breath, but she wasn't sure if she was that successful, especially after Eleanor appeared in the doorframe and made a specific remark. "You look like the cat that ate the cream."

"Hello, Grandmother," Genevieve replied, but she was careful not to admit the reason for her smirk.

Eleanor turned to her husband. "George, I need your kind assistance on a particular matter. Won't you join me in the study for a moment?"

Genevieve thought she heard him mutter something about "blasted women," before he reluctantly got up and toddled after her. Once he was gone, she glanced across at his chair and tossed aside the paper she was reading. She jumped out of her seat and snatched the paper tucked securely in the side cushion. She read to discover it was an invitation to some sort of "Erotic-o-Rama" gala hosted by the Duke of Argyle at his estate just outside of the city.

Interesting. She tapped the card against her palm. Not only would this be the answer to her current malaise, but it might just be the opportunity to get the duke to finally notice her. She had long admired his handsome visage, but she doubted that he knew she was alive. However, if she attended this party, she was determined that by the time it concluded, he would.

A slow grin spread over her face. But then it froze.

It wasn't as though she could defile herself and court scandal on her own. She needed someone who could act as her accomplice.

And Genevieve knew just who to ask.

CHAPTER 2

A fortnight later...

"Erotic-o-rama? Really, Argyle, what were you thinking to come up with something so asinine?"

Cortland offered a tolerant smile as he sat in his library sipping a brandy and conversing with his long-time acquaintance, Griffin Barlowe, the Earl of Uxbridge. "What can I say, but I wanted to gain my guests' attention." He shrugged. "And Scottish whisky isn't something I should consume on a regular basis."

Griffin laughed. "I daresay I've done many a thing I'm not proud of when it comes to drink, but even I have my limits when it comes to naming an illicit house party."

He rolled his eyes as the earl exited the room. It wouldn't be long before the ladies from various London brothels began to arrive as the evening's entertainment. He'd asked these ladybirds specifically because this was to be the sort of event that would taint young debutante cheeks. He certainly didn't intend to have some haughty matron breathing down his neck at the first sign her charge might be ruined on some ridiculous accusation where he would find himself well and truly trapped.

Earlier, he had rifled through the acceptance letters that had arrived and noted that only one had sent their regrets—the Duke of Cranbrook. Cortland hadn't expected him to come, but he wouldn't have felt right if he excluded the man who had made it possible to don the WD signet ring, announcing that he was part of the alliance.

He always slept soundly, knowing that it was close at hand, secured in his desk at this very moment. He never traveled without it, and it gave him a sense of comfort in knowing that it was there at a moment's notice.

"Your Grace, the... other guests have arrived."

That was what Cortland adored about his butler. He never batted an eyelash, no matter what sort of opponent he was up against.

"Very good. I will greet them personally. Feel free to take what is left of the night off with pay and instruct the rest of the servants to do the same."

"Your Grace." He bowed. "That is very generous of you."

He withdrew a handful of coins and handed them to the butler. "Distribute these as necessary. And remember that all I ask for in return is loyalty. And discretion."

"It will be done, Your Grace."

Cortland had to chuckle, because the man was practically salivating with the money he'd just been gifted.

With any luck, by the end of the night, Cortland would be salivating for a different reason entirely.

~

"I'm not sure about this..."

Genevieve rolled her eyes at the hesitant note in her friend, Lady Arietta Greenville's voice. In turn, she feared that they had come all this way in a hired hackney, just to be forced to turn around and go home. She took her friend's hands in hers. "Come on, Etta. Live a little."

They had taken a risk as it was, because both of the girls had mentioned spending the night at the other's respective households. They might have been grown women out in society, but since they had been friends for a long time, their parents' estates bordering each other, no one had seemed to question the legitimacy of their claimed plan.

As they had each left their homes, they had veered away from their course and met at a specified location and time, where they had hailed a hackney and headed for the Duke of Argyle's estate, but more importantly, his fanciful house party. Genevieve glanced at the lights illuminating the darkness outside and heard the laughter coming from inside and couldn't wait to join the fun. The issue was convincing Arietta not to back out after they had come this far.

Although she hadn't wanted to deceive her, she couldn't resist dangling a carrot in front of her. Just as Genevieve had yearned to gain the attention of the Duke of Argyle, Arietta had felt the same for a certain gentleman as well. "You know," she said slowly. "I heard that the Earl of Uxbridge might be here."

As suspected, Arietta's eyes widened. "Do you think so?"

Genevieve nodded as she crossed her fingers behind her back and prayed that she wouldn't be struck down by a rare bolt of lightning for lying so effortlessly. "I have it on very good authority."

Arietta's brown eyes abruptly brightened, and her blonde hair appeared to shimmer in the candlelight coming through the windows. She grabbed Genevieve's hand. "What are you waiting for? Let's go!"

Genevieve laughed at her sudden enthusiasm. She turned back to the driver and said, "Wait for us. We shouldn't be more than a few hours." She tossed a sovereign at him, and he touched the brim of his hat.

She offered her arm to Arietta, and together they braved the front steps.

They waited for a moment for the door to open, but when it didn't, Genevieve used the knocker. After a short wait, it opened to reveal a gentleman with tousled dark hair and a lopsided grin on his face. A half nude female hung on to his arm, and it was readily apparent that she was not a society lady.

"Are you 'ere for the party?" he slurred.

For the first time, Genevieve wondered if she'd made a mistake. She had imagined a Cyprian's Ball, but she wondered if this went further than that. Past a bit of flirtation and straight to the bedchamber. "Er... perhaps. We—"

Genevieve didn't get to say anything else as her arm was grabbed and she was pulled into the den of iniquity.

Once she was inside, the scents of opium and alcohol assailed her nostrils, making her eyes water. There was also so much smoke in the air that she wondered if there was a fire somewhere. She glanced at Arietta and noticed she had paled. Genevieve imagined that her thoughts mirrored hers but were infinitely more terrible.

She urgently tugged on her arm. "Vivy, I think we should go," she whispered.

Instead of replying, the man who had opened the door and was acting as the current butler, released his companion and put an arm around both of their shoulders. "Come in an' stay awhile."

With his face so close to hers, Genevieve nearly gagged at the mixture of smells on his breath. "I think perhaps we made a mistake—"

"Nonshenshe." He ushered them farther into the house, and Genevieve thought Arietta might actually faint. She gave her friend a brisk squeeze of her hand, eliciting a nod as Etta temporarily snapped out of her haze.

However, when they turned a corner and entered the parlor, even Genevieve wasn't prepared for the sight of so many writhing, nude bodies draped over every single piece of furniture, against the wall, and even sprawled out on the floor. She'd heard of things called orgies, but she had never actually witnessed it firsthand.

"Oh. My…"

At first Genevieve wasn't sure if she had uttered the syllables, or if it was Arietta, but when she turned and saw her friend's ashen face, her eyes rolling back in her head, she knew things were about to take a drastic turn for the worst.

"Etta!" she gasped as she started to collapse. But Arietta was caught by a pair of strong arms. Genevieve glanced up at the rescuer and realized that he was far from being the hero of old. This man was dangerous incarnate, and the host of the party.

∼

CORTLAND WAS FURIOUS. No, more than that. He was absolutely livid.

But since he couldn't very well throttle the lady before him, considering who her relation was, he had to content himself with scaring her away. But first, he needed to get her away from the multitude of sexually aroused men with eager cocks all around them.

"I think you stumbled into the wrong party, Lady Genevieve."

Her hazel eyes widened. "You know who I am?"

"Yes," he clipped, hoping she caught the disapproval in his tone. "Why don't we chat after we get your unconscious friend somewhere safe?" He picked Arietta up in his arms and carried her across the hall to the library where, earlier, he'd been dreaming of a licentious evening. Instead, he feared that his Erotic-o-rama would end up being a Scandal-o-rama.

He laid the woman in his arms down on the settee and walked back to the door.

"Where are you going?" Lady Genevieve asked.

Rather than answer, he headed toward the conservatory where he gathered a pawpaw fruit. He returned to the library where he cut open the tropical plant and held it beneath the unconscious woman's nose. With a unique scent similar to fermented grapes, he had learned that it worked as an alternative to smelling salts. Her eyes popped open, and she put a hand to her forehead.

Lady Genevieve gasped and uttered, "That's remarkable," before she walked over to her friend's side. "Etta? Are you well? Can you hear me?"

It was difficult for her to speak, so Cortland walked over to the sideboard and poured a sherry for her, which he brought back to his patient. "Drink this," he instructed. She did so without complaint.

Lady Genevieve, on the other hand, wasn't so compliant. "Must you be so rude?"

He turned to her with a dry glare. "I am merely trying to get her back on her feet so that you both may leave."

She stiffened. "What if we don't want to go?"

He snorted. "Are you honestly prepared to engage in the activities that you witnessed in there?" he asked.

"If it's good enough for them, then surely it's good enough for me."

Cortland frowned. For some reason, the idea that she would take a gentleman up on his offer of a torrid affair didn't settle well with him. But he dared not examine why that might be. "Not tonight, it isn't. You're going home, and hopefully, no one is sober enough to remember your foolishness, so that your reputation might be salvaged on the morrow."

"What if I'm tired of doing what is always expected of me?"

He glared at her, but she didn't seem fazed.

"I want to experience life, not watch as it passes me by. Is it so wrong to dream of something... more?"

Cortland had to tell himself that she wasn't challenging him, she was merely speaking her thoughts aloud. And yet...

There was just the two of them here, other than her friend, who would likely take any of Lady Genevieve's secrets to her grave. He took a step toward her, and although she didn't flinch, he noted that she did glance at him warily. "Exactly how much *more* do you want, my lady?"

He had intended only to provoke her, perhaps tease her a bit, and send her on her way, so it was surprising when she turned the tables and shored her courage in front of his eyes and said, "This."

She lifted her arms and wound them around his neck and placed her lips firmly on his.

CHAPTER 3

In all her one and twenty years of life, Genevieve had never acted so boldly. Granted, she had dreamed about acting on her impulses more than once, but her upbringing and her need to act properly for her two younger siblings had always surpassed her desires.

But not tonight. In the midst of this revelry, she had made the decision to release her inhibitions and be... free with the one man she had pined for. The man she had yearned to notice her. Although her actions now might not do much more than annoy him, at least it was better than being ignored completely.

"Argyle, I daresay you 'aven't joined in the festivities—"

The slurred, masculine voice broke off when he realized that the duke was engaged. Genevieve was placed firmly away from Argyle. Scalding heat rushed to her cheeks, a mixture of embarrassment and being cast aside so easily with mortification that she had dared to show her emotions so effortlessly.

As the duke spoke to the newcomer, his back to the women, likely to shield them from the other man's view, Genevieve found the opportunity to slip away. Arietta was wide awake at this point, so Genevieve moved to the settee and grasped her hand. "We need to go," she whispered urgently.

Etta nodded and jumped up from the cushions as if they were on fire. Since the solitary doorway leading to freedom was blocked, Genevieve had already spied another way out. The window was open, letting in some fresh air, and she hastily rushed toward it, grateful that they were on the lower level of the manor. She wasn't sure if Etta would balk at lifting her skirts and throwing her leg over the sill in a similar manner, but she was right behind Genevieve as they sprinted across the lawn, hand in hand.

They rushed to the hackney and practically vaulted inside, and Genevieve shouted to the driver, "Go!"

He flicked the reins and they were off.

Etta put a hand to her heart, that was likely pounding as loud as Genevieve's and said, "Remind me never to engage in any of your plans again, Vivy."

Genevieve took one glance at her friend, slouched on the other side of the carriage, with her frazzled blonde hair and skirts a bit mussed, and started to chuckle. Etta's lips reluctantly twitched and they soon burst into giggles that eventually erupted into full out belly laughs. "You have to admit it was an adventure!" Genevieve said when she was finally able to take a breath.

"Indeed. And I'm quite content never to embark on another."

They fell into another round of laughter, but as their merriment subsided, Genevieve couldn't resist one last glance at the manor.

As they turned a corner of the long drive, she was able to catch a glimpse of the grandly lit estate. Her breath caught, because she didn't know if it was just the shadows of the night playing tricks on her, or if there was the silhouette of someone leaning against the railing near the front door.

Either way, she liked to imagine it was the latter, that she had finally caught the attention of the duke and that he would find it difficult to forget her after this night.

She leaned her head back against the squabs and closed her eyes with a dreamy smile on her face.

~

THE DUKE WATCHED the hackney ramble down the long drive with a scowl on his face. It would be some time before he would forget the maddening Lady Genevieve, and should she decide to grow a conscience and become forthcoming with her actions, he knew where his neck would end up—in the parson's noose. Even now, he could feel the chains of marriage beginning to tighten around his neck.

It was time for a drink.

He stalked back to the library and slammed the door in annoyance behind him. A pleasurable night had been effectively ruined by the arrival of two society chits searching for a good time. He poured a generous amount of brandy and shook his head. *Absolute rubbish.*

Although he didn't begrudge a lady testing her limits, and especially exploring her sexuality, he did find fault with her doing it as *his* expense. There was no doubt that should he find himself on the way to the altar, his ring would do no good when it came to the Duke of Cranbrook's blasted granddaughter. He could almost hear the deafening cries of babies in the nursery now.

Shuddering, he sank down into a nearby chair and rubbed at his temples. This was quickly spiraling into a personal nightmare where he didn't see any good outcome from it. He feared he was well and truly trapped after all, and through no fault of his own.

And that dreadful kiss she'd given him. He groaned at the pure innocence of it. He preferred his women to be experienced in the art of pleasing a man, not some fumbling virgin who blushed at the prospect of disrobing in front of anyone. He also preferred women vastly different from Lady Genevieve—buxom, blonde, and comely. While he begrudgingly admitted that she wasn't terrible to look at, her hair was dark, almost brown, and her eyes were hazel, just like her grandfather's.

Abruptly, Cortland's stomach revolted. Would he picture the Duke of Cranbrook every time they had to lay together? Bile rose in his throat, and he had to swallow several times before it subsided.

He shot to his feet and began to pace the room. He supposed it was settled.

There was nothing he could do but make the same terrible mistake his father had and offer for a woman who was completely unsuited to him. No doubt the affairs would start with Lady Genevieve as soon as the requisite heir was birthed and he would become a cuckhold like his sire, but he couldn't risk the chance that he would lose membership in the alliance. Unfortunately, he also knew the ring would not be of any use to him this time, considering the lady he wished to escape was the founding duke's granddaughter.

He abruptly paused. Perhaps he could turn all of this chaos around to his favor. If the Duke of Cranbrook was his in-law, then he would certainly be assured he was never in danger of losing his membership to the Wayward Dukes. He could enjoy life as before, but rest easy knowing that he was always spared from any sort of upheavel from his fellow members. No doubt one of his comrades would be able to placate Genevieve while he ventured out.

His sour mood began to improve. This might be the beginning of a wonderful association. The only impediment at this point was his future wife. If they married, she would have to learn a few tips about kissing—among other things.

And he supposed the duty fell to him to teach her.

GENEVIEVE HAD THOUGHT of the perfect plan to sneak out of the house, but not exactly how she might return. Not only had she considered the fact she might make it back earlier than dawn, where she could enter the house with no one the wiser, but when it came to breaking into her grandfather's house, she found the task a bit more complicated.

"Blasted lock." She didn't know how thieves managed this so effortlessly, when it was anything but quick or easy when she attempted the task. At least she knew that if marriage wasn't in the cards for her, she couldn't make a living as a common burglar. Probably not a pickpocket either.

She prayed that Etta hadn't had the same trouble when she'd dropped her off, but then, she'd likely had the foresight to take an extra key with her. Her friend was resourceful when she put her mind to it.

When the mechanism inside the lock finally turned with the assistance of her hair pin, Genevieve breathed a sigh of relief. "Finally." She opened the door that led into the kitchens and quietly shut it behind her, then firmly turned the lock with a sigh of relief. But she still had to make her ways to her rooms.

Tiptoeing up the back stairs, she was careful to avoid the ones that creaked the loudest. She didn't fully release her breath until she had entered her chamber and shut the door behind her. Genevieve quickly stripped off her clothes and climbed into bed.

She wasn't sure how she might ever sleep with her mind whirling as it was, but somehow she must have managed it, because she was awoken by the sound of her grandmother's exuberant voice what seemed to be only a short time later. "Time to rise, dear. There is a special guest downstairs waiting to speak with you." She shook her head with a tsk as Genevieve's ladies' maid threw open the drapes to let in the early morning light.

Genevieve groaned and put a hand over her grainy eyes. "Must I entertain now?"

"It's nearly eleven o'clock. Much too late to be lazing in bed all day."

Cracking open an eyelid, Genevieve saw the Duchess of Cranbrook moving to Genevieve's wardrobe. She couldn't hear the entire conversation between her and the maid, but she caught snippets. It was enough that Genevieve abruptly awakened. "No, no. We don't have enough time for a bath.... She will have to spritz some perfume... We must ensure she looks resplendent.... Argyle is not known as a patient man..."

It was the last that caused Genevieve to sit up straight in alarm. Surely the Duke of Argyle wasn't downstairs! She knew that he was friendly acquaintances with her grandsire, but the fact that *she* was getting made ready in such haste made her blood rush through her veins.

She must have uttered something about the duke, because Eleanor's head turned sharply back to her. "I have your attention now, don't I?" she snapped. "You don't want to keep a potential suitor like that waiting overlong. He might lose interest and leave. He is your first prospect in some time, after you declined the attentions of the Earl of Somerhaven."

"He was nearly fifty," Genevieve pointed out offhandedly. Her attention was rather fixated on the fact that her grandmother was calling Argyle a *suitor*. Surely she was mistaken.

Or, could it be, that she'd made more of an impression on him than she'd thought last night?

With a slight squeal of excitement, any weariness quickly dissipating, Genevieve got up and dressed in record time. She sailed down the stairs, but paused before she entered the parlor, because she didn't want to appear *that* eager to see him again.

Smoothing down her dress and patting her coiffure, to make sure it was still firmly in place, she walked forward in a demure fashion. Once she entered, her grandsire and the duke rose, although her grandmother merely smiled in approval.

Genevieve dipped into a deep curtsy. "Your Grace. What a lovely surprise."

When she rose, he looked at her as if annoyed. She had to be mistaken, of course. If he was enamored with her, as she thought, then it was likely just a look of pure delight. But he didn't want to be too obvious, so he had to appear circumspect in the opposite manner. She smiled at him and offered a wink meant to be conspiratorial, but he merely scowled further. He remained standing, while her grandfather resumed his seat.

"Lady Genevieve, I have come by this morning with a proposal of marriage, which your grandfather has kindly granted."

She froze. She certainly hadn't been expecting that. Had it been love at first sight when he'd finally noticed her? Either way, she wasn't quite ready to skip down the aisle just yet. In order for her to feel secure in their union, she needed some sort of affirmation of his affection. "You honor me, Your Grace, but might I have some time to consider—"

"Nonsense," her grandfather said gruffly. "This is a good match, Vivy. You should not hold any reservations about accepting Argyle."

And yet, she did. She cleared her throat delicately. "Might the duke and I converse in private for a moment?"

Her grandfather narrowed his eyes, but his wife rose elegantly from her seat. "Of course, dear. But only for a few minutes. We don't need to combat a scandal before the vows are spoken."

As they left the room, enclosing Genevieve inside with her future betrothed, she clasped her hands before her and regarded the man still glaring at her. "I would like to think that you are here under some sort of emotional attachment, Your Grace, but something tells me that's not entirely true."

"You would be correct," he concurred evenly. He leaned on

the mantel but set one hand on his hip. "You interrupted a particularly riveting gala last evening, and since I can't promise that no one might have been sober long enough to recognize you, I decided to lessen the damage by marrying you."

Genevieve tried to picture how any of that sounded like some sort of declaration, but since she couldn't fit any of his staid speech into that category, she lifted her chin slightly. "So you were in no way... struck by our encounter?"

He snorted. "Only in the most aggravating sense, I assure you. After you and your friend departed, I was not in the right state of mind to engage in various activities."

Genevieve's ire was starting to spark. She crossed her arms. "Yes, I can imagine it was quite a shame to fully appreciate your Erotic-o-rama after that." She rolled her eyes. "Really, Your Grace, couldn't you have come up with something a bit less childish?"

He lifted a brow, her barb appearing to miss its mark. "What do you even know about it, as innocent as you are?"

"Nothing, really." She shrugged. "But neither did it appear very appealing."

"That's because you don't understand the pleasure to be had."

He sounded completely bored now, and she had to keep from clenching her firsts in irritation. For someone she had long admired from afar, he was turning out to be a conceited ass. "Oh, yes. Forgive me for not seeing the fun to be had in riding someone around the parlor as if they were a pony." She tapped her chin in consideration. "But now that you mention it, he was hung particularly well. Perhaps I should have offered my kiss to him instead."

She waited to see if her bluff would work.

It did, but not in the way she'd hoped. "I wish you had so it would have saved me the trouble of being here this morning."

She batted her lashes at him. "My, Your Grace. How you flatter with your charming words."

He exhaled heavily. "Let's cut the pretense, shall we? I'll secure a special license to marry from the archbishop this morning and by tomorrow we can start our life of wedded bliss." He started for the door.

It wasn't until he'd passed her that she said, "Don't bother, Your Grace, because I don't intend on accepting your proposal, however lovely it might have been." She offered him her most brilliant smile. "Now, if you will excuse me—"

"Don't be ridiculous," he snapped. "Your grandfather already gave his consent."

"Yes, he did." She walked right up to him and lifted her chin. "But unless he wishes to haul me to the altar kicking and screaming, there will be *no* ceremony. Good day, Your Grace." She backed away and swept out of the room without another glance back.

CHAPTER 4

Cortland had never had the misfortune of meeting such an irritating female in his life. If he had, he would have certainly taken care to steer clear of her.

He walked in the front door of White's and barked an order for a glass of Scottish whisky. He had told himself not to drink any more of the stuff, but after the meeting he'd just had, he needed the fortitude to calm his temper.

Who was *she* to decline such a generous offer? He was the one making the sacrifice to ensure she didn't suffer any ill treatment from attending his gala, and yet, she would make it appear as though he was the villain. Truly, she was the most ungrateful wench he'd had the discourtesy of ever meeting.

He tossed back the first dram of whisky and ordered another, and then a third, until he finally requested the entire bottle to be placed at his table. Hopefully, by the time he'd finished with it, he could get the sour taste of Lady Genevieve out of his system. No doubt the Duke of Cranbrook would support his suit and they could be done with this madness sooner, rather than later.

"Rough morning?"

Cortland glanced up and had to reach out a hand to steady

himself, because the room abruptly began to spin. He narrowed his gaze and eventually, the Earl of Uxbridge's face came into focus. "Ah. Join me. Join me." He kicked out a chair in invitation and Griffin shook his head.

With a rueful smile, Uxbridge murmured in return, "Are you sure it's safe?"

Cortland couldn't help but bark out a laugh. "I can't guarantee anything, old chap. Especially after this morning's fiasco."

"Do tell," the earl said dryly, as the waiter came over bringing his usual port.

Leaning forward, as if imparting a great secret, Cortland spoke with a bleary-eyed stare. "I dared to try to do the right thing by the St. Giles chit, and do you know what she did?"

"I am all agog," Griffin murmured.

"*She* declined my proposal of marriage when I was only doing it to salvage *her* reputation."

Griffin snorted. "No doubt you approached her with your usual aplomb, so I can't imagine why she refused you."

Cortland pointed a finger at him. "Exactly my point! She should have been on her knees, grateful that I was making such a sacrifice on her behalf, but instead, she had the nerve to turn her back on me and walk out of the room! Can you believe that?"

"Indeed. It is difficult to imagine such a scenario."

Cortland nodded his head, satisfied that someone could see how unreasonable the gel was being. "With a snap of her fingers, she could hold her own duchess title, and yet, she had walked away. I daresay I am finished with trying to do any further good deeds if this is how I am to be treated."

"You mean, like a man who expects the lady to be grateful for your proposal?"

"Yes." Cortland frowned, as his statement pierced the fog surrounding his pickled brain. "No. Wait. I'm confused. What are you saying?"

"Merely that you might have better luck with the lady if you tried a bit of courtship."

Cortland jerked as if the earl had suggested he bathe in a tub full of leeches. "Are you mad? I don't fancy the chit. I was merely trying to do the honorable thing."

Griffin tapped a hand on the table. "Perhaps what you should do, Argyle, is wait and see if rumors start to swirl about her. If not, then more than likely her reputation is sound and you won't have to worry about your gentlemanly duty at all."

"Indeed." Cortland's mind cleared as quickly as if the sun had shone brightly from beneath a cover of clouds. "Why, that is brilliant, Uxbridge. I daresay I should have considered that before I made an utter cake of her." He laughed in relief. "It's a good thing I have your council to rely upon."

"Quite." The earl cleared his throat as he downed his port. "If you will excuse me, I have an appointment I can't miss. I shall bid you good day and good luck."

"I shan't need luck now, old chap!" Cortland called after the man's retreating back. "The only thing I need is to retain my freedom, and I shall do so now that you have given me much to ponder!"

Cortland decided that it was time for him to depart as well. There was a ball that he was expected to attend that evening. Or at least, he needed to make an appearance since it was being held for one of the alliance members. One of the married ones, poor sod. But he wanted to ensure that his new duchess had a successful gathering, so he intended to do his part to ensure it was well attended. A party with one duke was considered to be a boon, but with more than one, the matrons of society would be clamoring to gain future invitations in the off chance they might spot one of these rare creatures in the wild. And perhaps throw their eligible daughter in their direction.

He shuddered at the imagining and stood then promptly wavered on his feet.

And crashed to the floor.

~

GENEVIEVE WAS grateful to have a reprieve from the war taking place in the midst of the Cranbrook household. Her grandfather hadn't batted an eyelash when she had announced that she would not be accepting the Duke of Argyle, but her grandmother, on the other hand, had done everything short of threatening to send her back to the country until she came to her senses and married the man. It didn't matter what Genevieve said to defend herself, it was taken as an argument by an unruly child, even though she had reached her majority, and was quite able to make her own choices.

When Eleanor had mentioned the ball that evening, Genevieve had voiced the desire to go. Although she despised most *ton* events, because they were perfectly staid and boring, she desperately needed the escape that it would give her. She might be forced to travel in close proximity to the duchess in the carriage on the way there and back, but everything in between could be spent taking the air on the terrace or escaping somewhere equally quiet.

When they arrived, they handed their wraps over to the waiting footman. A sudden attack of nerves struck Genevieve as they waited to be announced, because what if Argyle was there? Would he approach her? Or pretend indifference? Perhaps act as though she was no one of consequence at all, just as he had done before the night of his house party.

In hindsight, she realized that she preferred being ignored, rather than suffering the arrogant aristocrat that he'd been that morning.

Her hands clenched as she thought of his crass approach to marriage and spending the rest of their lives together. It was like a business arrangement, only worse. The bubble of fantasy that she had spun, imagining that he had been pining for her all that time, had abruptly burst, leaving a sour taste in her mouth.

She was quite sure that *nothing* he did could persuade her to change her mind.

After greeting their host and hostess, Genevieve patted her hair, to ensure the coiffure was firmly in place, and ran her hands down her light pink gown with its delicate, moss green, floral overlay. She'd had it designed especially for a special gathering because she knew that the colors complemented her fair coloring.

She certainly hadn't worn it for the Duke of Argyle. If she had, it was only to show him what he might have had, should he have approached her in a different manner.

Keeping her chin held high and proud, her footsteps sure, she entered the crowded ballroom with the confidence born of a duke's granddaughter. She glanced at her grandmother, and the duchess gave her nod of approval. If she were to be granted any olive branch this evening, that was likely it.

They parted at the foot of the stairs, and as Genevieve meandered about the edge of the ballroom, she told herself she was merely searching for Arietta, or another lady of her acquaintance.

But as she passed by the open terrace doors, her arm was grasped and she was pulled into the night air before she could gather her wits enough to scream. However, when she found herself in close proximity to the Duke of Argyle, her reservations quickly fled, to be replaced by something infinitely more dangerous. And perhaps even a bit wicked.

"Good evening, Lady Genevieve." His voice was huskier than usual, and his breath held a combination of mint and something darker, stronger. Even his cologne enveloped her in its scent. If it was possible to smell of desire and seduction, then surely he was the epitome of both.

"Your Grace." She had hoped to relay a flat rejoinder, but she feared it came out rather breathless instead.

He pulled her close. "I was hoping we might have a chance to talk."

In the light of the full moon shining down on them, she noted the color of his hair. She had always thought it was brown, but it was actually more of a chestnut red. His eyes were deep and brown with tiny flecks of gold, that matched his brown waistcoat and black attire to perfection.

But then she noticed the slight discoloration near his temple.

Genevieve frowned. "What happened to you?" She gently touched the bruise.

"Ow!" He jumped back as if he'd been burned. "I had a slight altercation with the table at White's this afternoon."

"Oh, I see." She crossed her arms in front of her. "You mean you got drunk and fell down."

He gave a haughty sniff. "I suppose if you want to categorize it in laymen's terms."

She sighed. "And yet, you wonder why I didn't fall at your feet when you offered me your hand." She moved to the stone rail surrounding the terrace and glanced out at the darkened gardens beyond. It would be the perfect place for a late-night tryst. And perhaps, if she had initially conversed with Argyle under different circumstances, she might have been inclined to traverse those paths below. Instead, those illusions about how she would get him to notice her had been shattered, never to be rebuilt.

What a shame.

∽

As Cortland studied Lady Genevieve, he wondered what she was thinking. She looked so upset, dare he consider almost melancholy, that he had the sudden urge to draw her into his arms and comfort her. Not only that, but with the moon shining on her curls, turning them into a golden halo around her head, and the gentle curve of her face looking as soft as silk, he had to clench his fist to resist reaching out and running a fingertip along her delicate jawline.

He desperately searched for something to say, anything that would remove these dangerous thoughts from his mind and remind him that she was a ruthless female, intent on ruining the lives of men everywhere. But when he spoke, the first thing that popped into his head sounded quite ridiculous. "How did you get the nickname Vivy?"

She turned to face him, and he was struck by the brilliance of her hazel eyes yet again.

Cranbrook, he reminded himself sternly. They are the same.

And yet...

There was a particular, feminine spark in her gaze that his mentor, her grandfather, lacked.

"There's nothing special about it, if that's what you're asking. It's merely a shortened version of Genevieve. Why?"

"I just wondered." He shrugged and slowly moved forward until he'd joined her at the railing. Leaning against the stone, he relaxed his hands on the top and regarded her steadily. "It doesn't suit you."

The line between her brows deepened into a frown. For some reason, he found it utterly charming. "How would you know what suits me? You don't know me."

His gaze roamed over her face. "Oh, I think I know more about you than you might think. I know that you dream of adventure, otherwise, why would you sneak a peek at your grandfather's invitation and show up at my Erotic-o-rama?" He paused, giving her time for a rebuttal, but when she said nothing, he continued. "I know that you are strong and courageous, because when Lady Arietta collapsed from sheer fright, you didn't bat an eyelash and fall into hysterics like most would have. And I also know that instead of blushing and running out of the house that night, you were actually intrigued by what you saw."

"That's not true! I was horrified."

Cortland heard her claim to the contrary, but when she turned her head, refusing to meet his eyes, he knew she was lying. If that wasn't enough to prove it, her breathing had altered. "I don't believe you," he challenged.

She whipped her head back around to him. "You can speculate all you want, Your Grace, but I grow weary of your arrogant assumptions. I think I shall return to the ball."

He caught her arm and whispered in her ear, "I can introduce you to the carnal world you only glimpsed. All you have to do is say yes."

For an instant, Cortland thought he had convinced her to give in to him, but even though they were so close, enough that it wouldn't have taken much effort at all to kiss her thoroughly, until she was crying out his name, he wanted her to be the one to approach him.

"Good evening, Your Grace."

She pulled her arm free and stalked away from him.

CHAPTER 5

For the remainder of the evening, Genevieve couldn't rid herself of the duke's touch, or the shiver that came over her whenever she recalled his dark promise.

All you have to do is say yes...

She opened her fan and waved it in front of her face. No doubt she was flushed greatly and had all the appeal of a cooked lobster as she meandered around the perimeter of the ballroom. She had danced, of course, because she was the granddaughter of a duke, the daughter of a marquess, and the sister of an earl. She never lacked for partners because her presence was never ignored. Except by one man.

Until the fateful night she'd dared to risk her reputation and the threat of scandal. But now that she had his attention, it wasn't what she'd been expecting. She had imagined he would trail her about like a willing puppy, eager for a morsel of her attention, thus keeping her in control. Instead, Argyle was a man like no other. He was virile and bold, determined to get what he wanted. The problem was that Genevieve wouldn't be able to control a man like that. He would absorb everything that she was until *she* was the one following after him, desperate for a crumb of his affections. Because once she gave him what he wanted, it might be perfect for a time, but it would never last.

Even though he had offered marriage to her, it would have to be built on something more than lust. There would have to be a mutual respect, and right now, that was sadly lacking. Neither of them trusted the other. It would have to be earned, and until she could be assured that there was something that could withstand a firm relationship, she would have to keep her distance, no matter how much she might be tempted otherwise.

She walked over to the refreshment table and accepted a glass of Madeira from the footman. She needed something that would calm her nerves, because every time she caught Argyle's silhouette in the room, those eyes were boring into her.

She downed the wine in one, fortifying gulp.

"Take it easy, there." She jerked when someone spoke at her elbow, but her nerves quickly eased when she saw the Earl of Uxbridge. He gestured to the empty glass in her hand. "That has a way of sneaking up on you unaware. You wouldn't want to give anyone the opportunity to take advantage of you when you weren't in possession of all of your wits."

Genevieve wondered if that was a warning about the duke. She knew that they tended to frequent the same circles, as well as the same club. "Thank you for the cautionary, my lord."

As the sounds of a quadrille came to a close, he asked, "Is your dance card empty? I wondered if I might request the next set."

She blinked, but then recalled the small square hanging from her wrist. The next dance was a waltz. "It appears I'm free. It's all yours, Lord Uxbridge." She held up her arm, and he scratched his name in the blank. As he did so, she tried to imagine herself with him instead. He was quite appealing with his brown hair and sharp green eyes. He was even taller than Argyle. She actually had to recline her head to look up at him, whereas she stood nearly eye to eye with the duke. However, she had always known she wasn't petite, but more of a willowy frame.

As the musicians tuned their instruments, he held his arm out to her and she accepted the offering. When they took to the floor, she didn't dare seek out the duke, even to offer him a smug expression, but something told her he was lurking somewhere in the crowd. She could feel the fine hairs on the back of her neck tingle in awareness.

When the earl started to lead her across the floor, all she could think of was Argyle. She allowed her mind to imagine the two of them together in one of those torrid embraces she'd witnessed in his parlor. He would slowly remove her gown and kiss his way down her body. Although she was an innocent, she had read enough to know what happened between a man and a woman, but even then, she hadn't been prepared for the sight of those sweaty, writhing bodies. She grew warm just imagining being with Argyle in such an intimate fashion.

And when she pictured his mouth upon her breast, his strutting cock impaling her, it caused her to miss one of the steps in the dance and trod upon her partner's foot. "Pardon me," she muttered, embarrassed at being so clumsy.

Luckily, the earl was a strong partner, and he made it appear as though nothing untoward had happened. His smile was also kind and genuine. "Think nothing of it. I would be distracted if I was being pierced with daggers from Argyle." He paused and considered something over her shoulder. "Come to think of it, I might actually be the recipient."

This caught Genevieve's attention. "Are you quite sure?"

"Indeed. In fact, he's coming this way."

The blood drained from her face. "What?"

"Don't worry about it." The earl shrugged. "I've never known Argyle to care about any woman longer than one night. The fact you've got him this distraught says a lot in your favor."

"I'm not so sure about that."

"It is if you truly want to marry him."

Her eyes widened. "What makes you say that?"

His smile was gentle but knowing at the same time. "I've noticed your infatuation with Argyle, even if he's been blind to it until now. If you want to know the key to winning his heart, all you have to do is exactly what you've been doing. He can be quite persuasive when he's after something, but don't give in too quickly. If you do, the race will be over."

～

CORTLAND DIDN'T KNOW what Uxbridge had said to Genevieve to put that ashen expression on her face, but he didn't much care for it. "Mind if I cut in?" he said firmly, giving the earl a decided glare.

"By all means." The earl graciously conceded her to him, but not before a speaking glance passed between them.

When she offered a slight nod, and the earl walked away, Cortland took her into his arms and resumed the waltz. "Dare I ask what that was all about?"

She blinked. "I don't know what you mean. The earl was being very considerate." She rolled her eyes. "Which is more than I can say for you. Is it a habit of yours to ensure you make a scene at every possible opportunity?"

"Not at all," he returned smoothly. "My sole purpose in life, at least at the moment, is to merely bedevil you."

"For what purpose?" she said. "I haven't done anything to you."

"Haven't you?" He pulled her a bit closer than was proper. "If that were true, why do I wake every night with an aching cock and your name on my lips when I find my release?"

She swallowed. "Honestly, Your Grace, must you be so vulgar?"

"I'm only speaking the truth." His gaze eclipsed her from the top of her head to the tip of her toes. "What must I do to convince you to be mine? I promise that the pleasure alone would be worth it."

She tilted her head to the side and offered a tolerant smile. "I'm not sure I'm convinced about that, Your Grace. I've heard of your many exploits through the years in all the gossip sheets, but I find them quite farfetched. Perhaps even... fabricated?"

"The devil you say!" His exclamation turned the heads of a few passing dancers, so he lowered his voice. "If you wish to have a demonstration of my sexual fortitude, I would be more than happy to comply."

She dared to feign a yawn. "I find your continual boasting to be quite bothersome. If you wanted to prove yourself to me, how about doing so with patience and humility?"

His mouth went slack. "Are you serious?"

"Indeed." As the waltz drew to a close, they came to a halt, and he reluctantly released her. In truth, he'd enjoyed holding her in his arms. It was as if she was made just for him. "Let's put that theory to the test, shall we? If you truly wish to court me properly, then I propose you do so with all the necessary accoutrements that a gentleman needs to woo a lady. Flowers, chocolates, perhaps even promises that you don't intend to honor. After a brief period of time, if I feel you are succeeding, then I shall grant you a single kiss, but nothing more. Anything else will have to be earned."

This time, it was Cortland who blinked. "Are *you* serious?"

She lifted her pert little chin. "You've heard my terms, Your Grace. Accept them or don't. It's up to you, but if you wish to play by my rules, then I shall expect you at the Darlington musicale tomorrow evening."

She offered a brief curtsy and spun on her heel, her appealing backside taunting him as she sauntered away.

He muttered a curse under his breath. God save him from distracting females. He didn't know at what point he'd lost all control of Lady Genevieve, but it was time she learned he wouldn't be brought down so easily.

Pulling down the sleeves of his jacket, he strode off in the opposite direction.

∽

GENEVIEVE WOKE up the next morning and stretched in contentment. She had been confident when she left the ball last night that Argyle would have no choice but to abide by her demands, thus putting her back ahead in the game.

But when her maid entered with her breakfast tray and she asked if there had been any deliveries for her that morning, the girl had shaken her head. "I'm sorry, my lady, but there is nothing. Were you expecting anything?"

Genevieve's spirits fell. "No. Nothing." However, she quickly rallied. Perhaps it was too soon to expect much. She had thrown down a gauntlet at his feet, so it would take some time before he resigned himself to her demands. But surely a single rose wouldn't have been amiss.

She froze. What if she'd gone too far and he decided he was going to wash his hands of her?

Her heart started to pound with panic. This wouldn't do.

She quickly got out of bed and rang for her maid. She needed to stay busy so she wouldn't go mad thinking of the duke before this evening's festivities. Otherwise, it would be a very long day.

Before she dressed, she sent a note around to Arietta and waited anxiously for her reply. When it came, she sighed in relief. Thankfully, Etta didn't have other plans already, so she would be delighted to join Genevieve for a day of shopping. She added that she was in need of a new bonnet.

Genevieve clasped the reply to her chest in gratitude. Someday, she would owe her friend dearly for all of the times she had saved her, but for now, she was just eager to leave the house.

As she appeared downstairs, she encountered her grandmother. "You look lovely, dear. Where are you headed?"

"To Bond Street. With Lady Arietta."

"Oh, yes. The Marquess of Hillhouse's gel." She appeared to find no fault in that, but then she paused. "Have you reconsidered the Duke of Argyle's proposal yet? No doubt it will not stand forever, and I should hate for you to miss out on such an advantageous match."

She offered a tight smile. "Not yet. But I should have my answer very soon."

"Very well." The duchess shook her head but said no more on the subject as she walked away.

Genevieve was grateful for it, because she wasn't sure what to say anymore when it came to Argyle. She had thought she'd had his arrogance boxed into a corner, but now she wondered if she had any sort of sway with him at all. If she didn't give him what he wanted initially, he might decide to turn another direction. Although she desired to take him down a peg or two, her grandmother was right. She didn't want to miss out on the chance to marry him, since she couldn't imagine herself with anyone else. He was the only man who made her stomach flutter with delicious excitement.

It was time to rethink her strategy.

~

THE DARLINGTON MUSICALE was half over by the time Cortland arrived. He was sure his tardiness would stick in Lady Genevieve's craw to know that he had purposely arrived late, when she was likely expecting him to be prompt and eager to engage with her. It was all part of his grand scheme of things to make her beg for *him*.

He smiled when he imagined the little pout she must be wearing on those luscious lips. It made him happy to think she had been fidgeting in her seat, awaiting the moment he might finally arrive.

Perhaps she'd even saved him a seat—

His thoughts came crashing to a halt, the grin wiped effectively from his face when he entered the room and saw her elegant coiffure in the midst of the assembled.

She wasn't alone.

To one side of her was the chit who had fainted at the first sight of the orgy in the parlor, but on the other was a gentleman Argyle didn't know. Yet.

However, it wasn't as though he could elbow his way across the aisle of chairs. With any luck, intermission would be close at hand and he would be able to confront his future bride and her new swain.

A short time later, fortune smiled on him as the last performer left the makeshift stage at the front of the room as refreshments were brought out by liveried footmen.

Lady Genevieve was smiling and chatting amicably with Mr. Irritation, as Cortland had taken to referring to him. However, when he made his presence known, her smile faltered and fell. While he hated to see it fade from her lovely face, the dark scowl that was likely imprinted on his face was likely the reason for her sudden apprehension. At least she was intelligent enough to sense his disapproval.

"Lady Genevieve, you haven't yet introduced me to—"

"The Duke of Argyle." The man was wide-eyed almost flustered, as if he was in the presence of Zeus himself. "It's an honor, Your Grace."

"Er, yes." He cleared his throat and tried again. "I'm afraid I didn't catch your name—"

The stranger laughed in return. "Oh, dear. I fear I suffer terrible adversity with proper conversation. I spend most of my time in the country, you see."

Cortland waited for more, but still, the man's identity

remained a mystery. It suddenly occurred to him why he might remain sequestered in the country. He could hardly string two words together.

"This is Lady Arietta's cousin, visiting from Brighton. Lord Henry—"

Lady Genevieve's introduction was cut short by the low bow from the man in question. "Greenville." He finished for her. "Lord Henry Greenville."

He smiled, as if absurdly pleased by the fact, and Cortland started to wonder if he had to be threatened by this man at all. If he wasn't mistaken, Lord Henry, with his curly blond hair and blue eyes, might prefer the company of other men. His lips twitched as he suppressed his merriment. In fact, he was quite sure of it.

His gaze shifted to Lady Genevieve, and he offered her a speaking glance that she must have appropriately interpreted, because her cheeks colored slightly. He turned back to Henry and offered the slightest of smiles. "Charmed."

To his surprise, Lord Henry's cheeks colored as well.

Yes, definitely no threat there when it came to Lady Genevieve. But he might have to take care to ensure *he* didn't give the wrong impression.

"Lady Genevieve. Might I have a word in private?"

He could see her visibly swallow as she glanced at Lady Arietta. "Of course, Your Grace." She snatched a biscuit from the tray the footman held and grasped it as if it might somehow shield her from him.

How adorable.

He placed a hand at the small of her back and steered her toward the foyer, but before they made it that far, he looked around and pulled her into a shadowed alcove beneath the stairs.

Keeping her captive, trapped against the wall at her back and his body in front of her, he said, "If your attempt this evening was

CHAPTER 6

How Genevieve had longed to hear those words come from the Duke of Argyle's lips. But she never imagined in a hundred years that they would actually be spoken.

When she had set out to reevaluate her plan regarding the duke, she hadn't been sure what to do. It wasn't until she'd arrived at Arietta's house and Henry had stridden down the steps with the desire to join them, that the idea had struck her to engage his services as her escort. Although she had been hoping that the duke might already be there when they entered, her arm looped though his, she'd been sorely disappointed. But then, she decided that must have been his alternate method of courting her.

Nevertheless, she'd found Lord Henry to be an animated partner and had things been different, she might have considered the possibility of a bit of flirtation. But she knew her efforts would have been wasted. It didn't take a scholar to discover that he preferred the company of his own sex. But he was kind and charming and took some of the sting out of Argyle's absence.

And when he'd finally appeared, the furious glare she'd noticed on his face had been worth all her efforts.

However, since she couldn't very well admit to it, she said, "I don't know what you mean, Your Grace."

He laughed darkly. "Come now, Lady Genevieve. We both know what your intentions were. It was the reason you pretended to hang on to your companion's every word, knowing that I might walk in and see you at any moment."

She snorted. "You hold your own self esteem entirely too high, Your Grace. Truth be told, Lord Henry is a very lovely man when it comes to conversing."

"He may be," he concurred. "But you will never get anywhere with him other than friendship. But with me—" He lifted his hand and ran the backs of his fingers down her cheek. She closed her eyes and leaned ever so slightly into the touch. "You can have it *all*."

She was wavering, yearning to be with him in every way that mattered. However, she recalled the earl's cautionary and opened her eyes as she forced herself to put her hands on his chest and move away from him. "I shall have to decline once again, Your Grace."

"I'm you're *betrothed*!"

Genevieve froze, halfway out of the alcove, as one of the biggest gossips in London passed by in that moment. Her brows lifted to her hairline as she glanced past Genevieve and spied the speaker behind her. Lady Avenly would have to be completely deaf not to have overheard the duke's claim.

When the lady turned a corner, Genevieve spun back around to him. "Now you've done it!" she hissed.

He pretended all innocence as he tossed her earlier words back at her. "I don't know what you mean, Lady Genevieve."

"Ooh!" She stomped away from him, returning to the musicale, not bothering to see if he had remained for the performance or not. With a few words, he had effectively sealed their fate.

CORTLAND WAS HALF-AFRAID to check the gossip columns in the paper the next morning, because something told him that Lady Genevieve was right. He knew Lady Avenly's reputation, her penchant for any sort of gossip that she could uncover, and considering he was caught alone with Lady Genevieve, in a secluded alcove, and boasted that he was her betrothed...

It was bound to end in disaster.

He opened the paper and flipped through the pages until he found what he'd been looking for. It was worse than he'd thought.

It is with good authority that this reporter proclaims an impending engagement between the Duke of Argyle and Lady Genevieve St. Giles. They were caught in a compromising position at the Darlington musicale last evening, which only begs the question – why has there yet to be an official announcement?

Blast. Cortland crumpled the paper in his fist and tossed it into the fire in his study. Reading the article, the accusation made it sound as though Genevieve was on the verge of being ruined, and that's what might prompt an engagement, instead of the fact he had been the one to offer for her first.

No doubt the other dragons in society would be eager to sink their claws into a lady with such a stellar reputation and impressive family ties.

There was no hope for it now. The game was over. It was straight to checkmate.

He called for his butler and scrawled two letters. One was sent to the Duke of Cranbrook, and the other was sent to Genevieve's father, Daniel St. Giles, the Marquess of Hollibrook, at his country estate. If he wished to be present for the marriage of his eldest child, then he would have to arrive by the following day. In light of an impending scandal that might besmirch the family name, it was imperative that they wed at the earliest opportunity to lessen any possible damage, rather than wait three weeks for the banns to be read.

He snatched his jacket from the back of a chair and shrugged into it as he waited for his horse to be saddled and made ready. It was time to pay a visit to the archbishop for that special license.

As he rode to the diocese, he finally thought of his mother, sequestered as she was in Scotland. He wavered whether he should even announce his nuptials but decided that she would read about it soon enough. He wasn't going to bother offering an olive branch, when he didn't care to mend that damaged relationship. As far as he was concerned, it would never be altered. He was content with never seeing her again.

He clenched his jaw. And yet, he was willingly on his way to get a legal document that would bind him to one woman for what remained of his days. He was taking that risk to be a cuckold when he'd promised himself he would never marry for just that reason.

Thus, he decided to pretend that he was doing this to spare the Duke of Cranbrook and his family any dismay that might arise. He was still a member of the Wayward Dukes, after all. He wanted to be an honorable member of the alliance. If that meant he had to give up his freedom to prove his loyalty, then that was what he would do.

~

GENEVIEVE STARED at the ceiling in her room. Her hair was styled and her gown perfectly pressed. Or rather, they had been, before she'd plopped down on the bed to await the arrival of her future husband.

She was going to be sick.

This was not the best way to win the duke's affections. In fact, it was the worst possible way. Not only would he despise her for trapping him into a marriage that she had tried to her best to *avoid*, but no doubt he would make her suffer the consequences from it.

She put a hand over her eyes. She had never heard anything bad about the duke's behavior, but what if he was the kind of man who raised a hand? She would never be able to tolerate that, and English law would certainly prohibit her from obtaining a divorce. A woman who married was her husband's property, as surely as his estate and his horse. The only way she could manage a legal separation was if he was found to be incompetent in the bedchamber, but his previous history with women would prove that invalid by several degrees.

No, she was well and truly trapped.

All you have to do is say yes...

Not for the first time, his dark promise flitted through her mind with all the delicious torment she had started to associate with him. They hadn't kissed properly, and yet, she was yearning for the night they would finally lay together as man and wife. While there might be a touch of maidenly reserve, it was eclipsed by that whispered taunt in her ear. Something told her that the Duke of Argyle would be a very generous lover.

But it was what sort of *husband* he might be that worried her.

She didn't open her eyes when the door opened and closed. Not until the maid said, "These just arrived for you, my lady," did she reluctantly crack open one of her lids slightly.

She quickly sat up when she caught sight of what the maid held.

Genevieve followed the elaborate bouquet with her gaze. It was so massive that she couldn't see the maid's face when she carried it over to her bedside table and placed it down gently. "Those are... breathtaking."

"Yes, my lady. I would agree." The maid glanced toward the small square in the midst of all the various hothouse blooms. "Perhaps you should read the card."

Genevieve reached out and plucked out the small paper and read the confident, masculine scrawl.

To my future bride.

I can't wait until you say yes.

Yours,

Cortland

It took Genevieve a moment to realize that he'd signed it with his given name rather than his ducal title. Had she bothered to think of what it was? She'd always just called him by his title or Your Grace, as was proper. It would be so strange to call him something so intimate, but she supposed she should get used to it. She would soon be his wife, after all.

She put a hand to her stomach, sure that she would retch.

"Oh, my lady, you look rather peaked. Are you feeling well?"

No. "Yes, I'm fine."

The maid smiled kindly. "No doubt it's just those bridal nerves. They hit every lady before they take their vows. I'll go down to the kitchens to see if cook has anything that might settle your stomach."

She bobbed a curtsy and left before Genevieve could tell her not to bother. Then again, perhaps it wouldn't be such a terrible idea.

A short time later, after the maid had returned with a strong peppermint concoction, Genevieve had to admit that it had helped somewhat. She was able to take a breath without feeling as though she needed to rush for the chamber pot.

However, that all changed when it was announced that her affianced was downstairs. She took several bracing breaths and told herself that there was nothing to fear. He was just a man with a title. He wasn't so different from her father who would someday, inherit the same. Just because they were getting married in three weeks didn't mean she wouldn't have time to get used to the idea.

She exhaled steadily. Thank goodness for banns.

Genevieve headed downstairs in another gown of light pink. When she entered the parlor, the duke and duchess were conspicuously absent. The only one present was Argyle.

Cortland, she mentally corrected herself. She tried to picture calling him that and couldn't quite picture it.

"Dare I ask what the reason for your sudden frown is? Surely it wasn't the flowers I sent?"

She blinked. "Not at all. They are very beautiful. I suppose I was just trying to get used to calling you by your given name."

"It's Cortland," he said dryly. "Go ahead and try it out. You might as well get used to it. You'll be screaming it soon enough."

Genevieve opened her mouth but found it as dry as dust. She cleared her throat and tried again. "Cortland."

He closed his eyes, as if savoring the sound. "Intoxicating." He opened his eyes and pierced her with that same dark, promising stare. "Genevieve." He lifted a brow and walked closer to her. "Or perhaps you would prefer Vivy?"

He paused directly in front of her. "Either is fine."

"Good." He smiled, and then drew her closer to him. "This time tomorrow, I won't have to ask permission to kiss you anymore."

Genevieve bristled at that. "Pardon me? Whether we are husband and wife or not, you will need to coerce me into your bed."

His eyes sparkled. "Oh, I intend to. Tomorrow can't get here soon enough."

Blinking in surprise, she had to speak up. "Pardon? We surely won't wed until the banns are properly read."

"Not really." He patted his jacket. "I was granted a special license just a few hours ago, so you had better prepare yourself to be called the Duchess of Argyle sooner rather than later, because in less than twenty-four hours, you will be mine."

CHAPTER 7

For an instant, Cortland wondered if she might fall at his feet, and not in the good way. She paled considerably, but surely she couldn't have been that surprised?

"I have taken the liberty of inviting your family to the wedding breakfast and—"

"What?" *Ah, that was better.* The color rushed back to her cheeks as her ire was sparked. "I didn't give you leave to do that."

"I'm to be your husband," he pointed out.

"But you aren't *yet*," she said. "Until the vows are spoken, I would like to think that I still have a bit of say when it comes to my parents and siblings. Especially when it comes to the fact I'm to be *married*."

Cortland finally paused. She appeared to be truly upset. He sobered his tone. "Forgive me. I was merely trying to get word to them as swiftly as possible."

Thankfully, she seemed to accept his apology, as her face softened slightly. "I understand you were doing what you thought was best. But I am not a hapless debutante who needs proper direction. I have been out in society for some time now, and before that, I was schooled to be the wife of an aristocrat. I can hold my own when necessary."

"I don't doubt that you can. In truth, I'm eager to see all that you can master."

Her cheeks colored slightly and although he used to despise blushing females, he found that, on her, a blush was rather... quaint. He wondered if she turned that delightful pink all over her body.

An overwhelming desire to kiss her struck him, but he couldn't do it in the middle of the parlor. Even if they were as good as wed at this point, they weren't yet, and no doubt the Duchess of Cranbrook would frown upon such forward behavior. "Take a walk in the gardens with me."

She eyed him warily, as if understanding the reasons for his request. "Why?"

He held out his arm. "Don't make me ask you twice."

Her lips twitched, her eyes narrowing, as if her stubborn nature and her curiosity were at war with one another. Finally, she threaded her arm through his. He offered her a broad grin of approval, and his breath caught when he looked into her fathomless, hazel eyes. He realized now how wrong he'd been to put such an unusual shade in the same category as that of her grandfather. She had a uniqueness all her own.

He quickly slid his gaze away as he led her outside in the warm sunshine. It was a perfect day with white fluffy clouds passing by in the brilliant, blue sky overhead. He couldn't have asked for a better day to fall in love.

He nearly faltered over his own feet. *Love?* Since when had such dangerous thoughts begin to taunt him? He desired, perhaps even lusted, after Lady Genevieve, but that was as far as it went. He wouldn't allow himself the weakness of succumbing to such an emotion as love. His father had claimed to love his mother: and look where that had gotten him: nothing but heartache.

Pushing aside such unsavory thoughts for the moment, he

concentrated on the gentle swell of her breasts beneath her décolletage and imagined the slender length of her legs as they wrapped around his waist. Soon, his mind was back on the right track. Amorous congress was something with which he was all too familiar and eager to engage in, even though it had been some time since he'd lain with anyone.

He stopped when they rounded a corner of the house. Standing next to a blooming rose bush, he gathered her into his arms. "I've been waiting for this moment for days," he whispered next to her temple. He pulled back slightly and asked, "Would it be acceptable for me to kiss you, Genevieve?"

Instead of answering, her lips parted slightly. It was enough of an invitation for him to engage.

∽

GENEVIEVE CLOSED her eyes as she waited for Cortland's mouth to brush hers.

It never came.

She slid open one lid and, keeping her lips pursed, she said, "Aren't you going to kiss me?"

He smiled in a tolerant manner and asked, "How many times have you kissed a man?"

"Other than the house party?"

He nodded.

She gave an unabashed smiled. "None?"

His eyes widened at this. "You've never snuck an embrace with anyone before?"

She shook her head, and then bit her lower lip, afraid that she had turned him away from her, but if anything, his brown gaze darkened even further.

He reached up and gently cupped her cheek. "Close your eyes. I'm going to teach you what it means to truly kiss a man."

A thrill of excitement shot through her, and she willingly

HOW TO ENSNARE THE PERFECT DUKE

complied, but when she would have pursed her lips, she felt his thumb smoothing it back out.

"Just relax and follow my lead."

"Like a waltz?" she asked, hopefully. That, she had mastered long ago.

"In a sense," he returned. "But much more enjoyable."

At long last, she was granted the sensation of his mouth upon hers. The pressure was slight at first. He began to move slightly, and at his suggestion, she tried to mimic his movements. Already, a tingling thrill was beginning in the pit of her stomach. That was certainly a different sensation from dancing.

He pulled away, and her eyes opened.

"Very good." He lifted a brow. "Are you ready to try something more advanced?"

That curiosity he had mentioned earlier strengthened and screamed at her. "I… suppose." She closed her eyes once more, and again, his lips were gentle as they touched hers, but this time, he dared to lick the seam of her mouth with the tip of his tongue. Surprised, she gasped, and he slid it inside her. When it touched hers, she made some sort of noise. It was like nothing she had ever made before, a combination of moan and sigh.

Daring to be bold in return, she hesitantly flicked her tongue forward and met his. There was something about the slick contact that made the little tingles inside of her turn heated, to the point where she started to gasp. She lifted her arms and wound them around his neck, and he pulled her even closer to him, until her breasts were in direct contact with his chest. The heat that had had been building turned into an inferno, and that was when he deepened the kiss. He seemed to consume her entirely, until she wasn't sure where he stopped and she began. She had never imagined she could be so connected to another person.

When they finally parted, she was reluctant to let him go. He smiled at her and said, "I think you'll do just fine."

It was the sound of his praise, as if she'd passed some sort of erotic test, that she took offense with. "Do you?" She sniffed. "I think you could use a bit of work."

Rather than getting upset, he laughed richly. "I'm more than confident in my prowess, my lady, so I fear your barbs are misplaced." His eyes glittered. "I was referring, not to your innocence, but to the passion racing through your veins. You will make a sublime lover."

She moved away from him. "I'm relieved to hear that I won't be a disappointment as a wife."

"Far from it," he said huskily. "I find I'm looking forward to tomorrow more than ever."

∼

When Cortland returned home from visiting his future bride, he stepped out of his carriage, only to have a flour sack slide over his head. He was picked up by more than two sets of hands and tossed none to ceremoniously into a different sort of conveyance.

Boiling mad, he ripped the covering off his head with a string of curses. "Bloody vagrants!" He paused when he spied the three men sitting across from him—the Earl of Uxbridge, the Marquess of Overhill, and the Viscount of Cristley.

Cortland's anger subsided when he realized he hadn't been set upon by thieves, but he was still annoyed at being handled in such a manner. He brushed at his jacket and smoothed the hair away from his forehead. "Do you mind telling me what that was all about?"

The marquess was the one who answered. "Uxbridge told us that you were to be married in the morning. It wouldn't be a ceremony unless the groom had a proper stag party the night before."

Considering Overhill and Cristley had been present at his Erotic-o-rama, he had a good idea of what the two libertines had in mind. Uxbridge, on the other hand, had also been present, but he'd declined to take part in the festivities, choosing instead to brood over a glass of brandy most of the night. He had the feeling that something was bothering the earl, but he hadn't had the chance to question him about what it might be as yet. And considering Cortland would be leaving for his estate the following afternoon to embark on a lengthy honeymoon, and tonight would be spent at many of the London pubs, he doubted he would find a chance to confront him in the near future. He just prayed that it wasn't something unforgiveable.

"Although I imagined it would be Uxbridge who would fall prey to the parson's trap before any of us." the viscount noted. "You were my last choice, Argyle. Lady Genevieve must be rather convincing, indeed." He waggled his brows. "Perhaps if you tire of her, I might give her a go?"

It wasn't often that Cortland allowed anything his licentious friends said to upset him. He generally let it all roll off him like water from a duck's back. He knew that they teased in good sport, even if most of the laughs were at his expense, or sometimes that of others in society.

But a slight to his future bride could not be allowed to stand. "I would be cautious what you say of the lady in my presence, Cristley."

The marquess gave a loud guffaw. "Oh, now, you've gone and done it! The infamous temper of the Duke of Argyle will soon be unleashed upon you if you dare to speak of his lady love again!"

The two of them continued to laugh, but Uxbridge remained oddly silent. Again, it was quite out of character for him. But then, it wasn't often that Cortland didn't join in the merriment as well. This time, he found that he couldn't stomach their jesting behavior. It caused him to rap on the top of the carriage, which wasted no time drawing to a halt.

"What are you about, Argyle?" the marquess asked with a

mocking expression. "Don't say you aren't interested in a bit of fun."

"Oh, I am," Cortland countered. "But I find that my pleasure is best had elsewhere." He started to climb out of the coach, but then he paused and glanced at the earl. "Care to join me, Uxbridge?"

The earl got up and followed suit. "I thought you'd never ask."

Once they had shut the door behind them, Cortland smacked the side of the carriage so that the driver knew that it was safe to continue on.

"You conveniently stopped at White's," the earl noted.

"Yes. Quite ingenious of me, wasn't it?" Cortland shook his head as he headed for the establishment that boasted the familiar bow window. "I admit that I find it difficult to stomach those two this evening. Is something wrong with me?"

The earl smiled as they walked in and took their seats. "I am beginning to wonder if it is the same affliction that affects me."

Cortland looked at him expectantly.

"Maturity," he clarified.

Cortland shuddered. "Heaven help us."

"Indeed," Uxbridge concurred. When the waiter came over to bring his usual port, he waited for the duke to give him his order.

"Better bring a bottle of your finest Scottish whisky." Cortland glanced at his companion. "The earl and I have much to discuss this evening."

~

GENEVIEVE NEEDED A DRINK.

After suffering a lengthy, and awkward discussion from her grandmother, about what to expect in the marriage bed, she found that she had more questions than answers. When Cortland had kissed her in the gardens, she was under the impression that he'd approved of her responses, but to hear the Duchess of Cranbrook talk, it would be best if she laid still and waited under cover of darkness for him to come to her.

"Under no circumstances must you act as though you are enjoying the act taking place. It would make the duke wonder whether you are chaste… or a common trollop."

Genevieve had listened as she had extolled all the virtues expected of a young lady, and then branched out even further into what she would have to do as the duchess of her own household. When her grandmother had started to speak of menus, Genevieve finally had to hold up a hand. "I'm sorry, but I'm confused."

"About what?" the duchess had blinked. "It's not that difficult to comprehend."

"Indeed not, if you are speaking of proper decorations for the front parlor, but I know all of that. I have been taught everything there is to know about running an aristocratic household."

"But a duchess has more responsibilities than that of a marchioness."

"I have no doubt that's true," Genevieve said slowly, trying to contain her composure. "But it's the bedchamber that I need further clarification on. You said I was to lay there and not move. Are you sure that's the way to do it?"

"My dear," her grandmother implored firmly. "I have been married for over forty years. I should know how things are done at this point."

Genevieve couldn't very well argue that point, but neither did it ease her conscience. The duke had acted one way, and yet, her grandmother was telling her something completely different. She sighed. She supposed she would just have to wait until the following night to comprehend everything that was expected of her.

For now, she intended to ease her nerves by sneaking into her grandfather's study for a glass of sherry. She wasn't accustomed to drinking spirits, but she needed something to help her sleep. It wasn't every day that she agreed to give up her freedom to a man she was about to wed. All of her life she'd felt like the property of her father, told how to sit and how to act, and now she would be doing the same. The pressure to be the perfect duchess for Argyle was not something she was particularly looking forward to doing.

The only thing she was remotely excited about was continuing their lesson in kissing, but if that was as good as it was going to get, according to her grandmother, she wasn't sure she was that thrilled after all.

She had just taken a fortifying sip of the sherry when a gruff voice spoke up behind her. "Whatever Eleanor said to you, I would caution you to ignore it all."

Surprised, Genevieve inhaled at the wrong time. The drink she'd been in the process of swallowing went the wrong way, and she collapsed in a fit of coughing.

The duke walked over and hit his hand on her back, which didn't help matters when she was trying to catch her breath again. She waved a hand and attempted to talk. It came out as a raspy, "I'll be fine."

"You sound like my mother-in-law. God rest her soul." He lumbered over to the seat beside the mantel and sat down.

Once Genevieve had contained herself, she walked over and sat down across from him. "Thank you."

"For what?"

"Trying to make me feel better." She reached out and took his hand and gave it a gentle squeeze. "I shall miss you after tomorrow. Nothing will be the same ever again."

"Things are meant to change," he noted. "Otherwise, it would be a sadly populated place."

She sat back heavily. Her grandmother would surely find fault in the way she was slouching, but her grandfather said nothing as she processed what he'd just said. "I hadn't given any thought to being a mother." She put a hand to her stomach, imagining it growing larger with a babe.

"The duke will require an heir. Surely you knew this."

"Of course, I did." She rolled her eyes. "I've just never imagined being a mother."

"You will do fine," he consoled her. "I can tell you care a lot for Argyle. Because of this, it will ease the transition. Just remember to always talk things through. Communication is key for any successful union."

"I will remember that." She got up and bussed a kiss on his cheek. "I should get to bed. Tomorrow is a big day."

As she headed to her room, she clenched her fists at her sides.

She prayed it wasn't going to be the biggest mistake of her life.

CHAPTER 8

Cortland woke up bleary eyed and half dressed in his bed. At first, he was afraid that he'd done something entirely foolish, but then he recalled the two bottles of whisky he'd had at White's with the earl. Although it became a bit fuzzy after that, at least he was home rather than waking up somewhere foreign, where it would be difficult to convince his bride that he hadn't done anything untoward before their wedding ceremony this morning.

At the reminder, he jumped up and peered at the clock on the mantel. *Bloody hell.* He would be lucky to make it to the breakfast on time. He grumbled beneath his breath as he rang for his servant. When his valet answered his summons, he began to bellow orders to whomever might listen.

In record time, he was soaking in a bath and drinking some foul concoction that he'd gotten from the kitchens to cure the dreaded after effects of his pounding head. What had ever possessed him to drink to excess when he knew he had a very important night ahead of him? He needed his full faculties to bring Lady Genevieve to the heights of pleasure. Unfortunately, with a lack of sleep, and the way his head was pounding with all the force of a hammer to his skull, he wasn't in much shape to do anything more than close his eyes and pray for some sort of relief.

Before he was quite ready to leave the bath, he was roused and dressed in formal black and white evening attire. His valet took care of shaving the stubble that covered his chin, and gave his hair a slight trim so that it wouldn't brush his collar.

All the while, he was getting primed and ready to say his vows, Cortland hoped that his stomach would settle itself and he would be able to perform with charisma and aplomb without disgracing himself.

When it was time to go to the Duke of Cranbrook's house, he wavered unsteadily on his feet for a moment, and then managed to make it down the steps of his townhouse without falling. He considered it a well-done feat on his part and decided that he would make it through this day unscathed after all.

He arrived at his destination a short time later and eagerly anticipated the moment he would see his lovely bride. He realized that he was anxious to see her, and the whisky had helped to dull his senses until they were reunited once again.

Cortland pasted a friendly smile on his face, that he hoped didn't resemble a grimace, as he was introduced to his in-laws, the Marquess and Marchioness of Hollibrook. He also met the current Earl of Brookfield, Lady Genevieve's brother, and her younger sister, Gabriella. They seemed like an agreeable family and vastly different from the parents he'd grown up with. Without his father or siblings, and considering he didn't speak to his mother, his side of the parlor would be quite empty, other than a handful of close friends, mainly the Earl of Uxbridge, and Mr. Brandt Clarke and his wife, Ada, whom had just recently wed.

If he were in wont of any advice in that corner, he knew where he would surely go.

Of course, his alliance ring was secure in his waistcoat pocket.

For a day he thought he would never have to actually endure, it was a source of comfort to him now.

The Duke and Duchess of Cranbrook were there, of course, speaking to the vicar, and Cortland strolled over to the latter to discuss the ceremony while he waited for his bride to appear.

The skin on the back of his neck began to prickle and he turned toward the doorway of the parlor.

And there she was.

His chest got tight at the sight of her. She looked as lovely as an angel in her pale blue gown. Her curly, light brown hair had been drawn up into an elegant chignon that framed her face with delicate ringlets. Her hazel eyes were direct and knowing as they glanced about the room.

But it wasn't until their gazes clashed that time itself ceased to exist.

～

GENEVIEVE HAD BEEN fearful that the duke might change his mind, or at the very least, be late in order to make her worry he might not appear. So she was grateful to see him standing by the vicar. His russet hair was brushed back from his forehead, and he was dressed impeccably.

She would have imagined herself to be the luckiest woman alive to obtain such a catch—if it wasn't for the sight of his bloodshot eyes. Her lips pursed in disapproval. Of course, he would ensure that he spent the last night of his single life drinking and carousing about the city. God only knew how many women he had flirted with while she was being lectured on the proper way to behave.

She curled her hands into fists and told herself that she would get nowhere by turning into a shrew the first day of their marriage. She would act as a lady should and tomorrow, she would find out exactly what had transpired. As it was, he looked as though he might not be able to remain upright for the entirety of the vows.

To her surprise, however, he managed to do so, and even his voice rang loud and clear when he promised to love and honor. She feared she would stumble over the part that claimed she must obey, but she was able to manage it without choking.

It was over almost as soon as it began. The vicar closed his Bible and took his leave while she looked down at the solitary gem on her finger. Argyle told her it had been passed down for generations from previous duchesses in the family, and now she was the lucky recipient of the opal. It caught the light of the candles from around the room and shone with a certain brilliance. For an instant, she started to panic, hypnotized by the symbol it represented, but she quickly pushed aside her reservations, and concentrated on visiting with her family instead.

Unfortunately, the duke's estate was on the opposite side of London from the one she had called home for so many years. At least she would see her family when they all returned for the season. It was only because of her boredom that Genevieve had come to the city earlier than the rest of them. Now, she wondered if she might have been better served staying in the country.

Then again, glancing at her husband across the dining table as he chatted with her father, she knew that life as his wife would always have some sort of adventure.

The question that remained was—would it benefit her?

All too soon, her time came to an end. Her trunks were loaded into the ducal coach, and Argyle held out his hand to her as he assisted her into the carriage. He'd told her earlier that it would take a few hours before they reached his estate, so she had planned to pass the time with the morning paper. She thought she might keep the clipping announcing her engagement.

As they set out, it abruptly struck her that she was Genevieve St. Giles no longer. She was Genevieve Beaumont, Duchess of

Argyle. Tears abruptly sprang to her eyes. Not only would she be unable to spend every summer with her parents ever again, believing for years that she would be the spinster of the household, her new named sounded so foreign. Undoubtedly, it would take some time to get used to it.

At least her husband would help with the transition.

She glanced up from the newsprint in her lap and saw that he was involved in a novel. Her lips quirked.

He seemed to have the feeling that he was being watched, because he looked up and said, "What is it?"

"Nothing." She shrugged. "I just never took you to be a reader."

He lifted a brow. "Did you imagined that I couldn't read, perhaps?"

She laughed. "I would like to point out that those are your words and not mine."

"Indeed." He gave her an admonishing stare, but the sparkle in his eyes belied any annoyance he might have wished to portray.

Genevieve leaned her head back against the squabs and found that a smile had spread across her face. Mayhap this wouldn't be such a terrible union, after all.

~

WHEN CORTLAND WAS ASSURED that his genteel wife was asleep, he set aside his book. He would much rather enjoy his lovely bride on the way to his estate, but he wouldn't shag her in the midst of his coach like some East End doxy. She deserved more than that from him.

Not only that, but his head was still pounding from a lack of sleep and too much Scottish devil. He knew it would be best if he tried to get some rest as well, but he wasn't sure his unruly cock would allow it. Ever since he'd seen Genevieve in that doorway, dressed in all her wedding finery, he'd been dealing with a rather painful arousal. It had subsided somewhat during the breakfast, but now it was aching as badly as his skull.

He leaned his head back and willed his body to sleep, since he planned to be up until the wee hours of the morning, but as much as he willed the peaceful oblivion to come, it eluded him.

Although he enjoyed reading about the animal kingdom through the eyes of French novelist, Georges Cuvier, he wasn't sure he could absorb any more anatomy, when he wanted to engage in his own studies with his new duchess.

It made him wonder, for the first time, what some of her likes and dislikes were. What if she despised everything that he enjoyed? Outside of the bedchamber, of course. In that regard, he had no hesitation they would make a perfect fit.

What if he uncovered some tasteless habits that drove him crazy? Even if she wasn't an unfaithful companion, the way his mother had been toward his father, there were certain aspects that he found quite abhorrent. Perhaps she slurped her tea? Or complained about the cold in the winter? Was she good at watercolors, but hated needlepoint?

He frowned. He didn't know her favorite color. Nor the sort of flower she liked, which was why he'd sent her a bouquet of everything the flower seller had suggested. He had been speaking of the language of flowers, but it might as well have been Greek. At least Cortland had understood that, but courtship had long since failed him.

He had to find out what she enjoyed, because he wanted to do something nice for her when they arrived at his estate. He definitely wanted her to have a better memory than the writhing parlor scene she'd encountered the first time she'd been there.

He wanted her to feel welcome, to acknowledge it as her home. Perhaps he would hire a designer to come later that week with various swatches of fabric for her to inspect. The entire estate could do with an update. He hesitated. What if her tastes veered toward the eclectic? He could do without a red and orange bedchamber. Maybe that was one he would suggest leaving as it was. And his study.

He tapped a finger on the side of his seat and considered that he would wait on the designer until they'd had a chance to talk things over first.

Yes, that definitely seemed like the better choice.

Cortland considered more similar prospects until the coach came to a halt.

With a yawn, Lady Genevieve covered her mouth with her gloved hand. "Have we arrived?"

He snapped out of his reverie and smiled. "Yes, we have. Shall I give you the full tour of your new home?"

She seemed apprehensive, all of a sudden, and he wondered if he'd been too hasty. But then, she pushed aside her hesitation and offered him a warm smile. "That would be lovely."

~

THE ENTIRE TIME her husband guided her through the massive estate, the only thing she could think of was those bodies in the parlor and how it might resemble her time with the duke that evening. Her blood rushed through her veins in anticipation. She had been quite fascinated with what she'd witnessed, so she hoped it was the on the agenda.

When they parted, he said he would come back to collect her at supper, but he would take his leave now to make sure she was settled comfortably. "If there is something you wish to change, we can discuss an altered color scheme."

Genevieve looked around the powder blue and white room and knew she wouldn't change a single thing about it. It was soothing to the eye. "It's perfectly acceptable as it is, Your Grace."

"Cortland," he corrected. "Let's leave the titles to formal events."

She nodded. "Of course. Forgive the oversight. Old habits are difficult to break."

When she said that, the strangest look crossed his face, but he recovered soon enough and left.

The first thing Genevieve did was try out the bed. She went over and plopped down on it with uninhibited joy. She had long dreamed about the duke's kiss in the gardens and wished to duplicate it at the earliest possible opportunity. She had thought he might accost her in the carriage, but when that didn't occur, she had pinned her hopes on when they'd arrived at the estate. Although he was amicable, he made no untoward advanced toward her. Even when she'd glanced at him hopefully as they strolled through the front parlor, he was careful not to meet her gaze.

If she didn't know he was already enamored with her sexually, she might have wondered if his ardor had cooled. But it must be that he thought she felt awkward to be strolling these halls again under vastly different circumstances. She would have to set his mind at ease on that score as soon as possible.

However, when she thought about approaching the subject at dinner, she decided that perhaps it wasn't the best time, because although they sat at the table alone, two footmen stood at the perimeter of the room, ready and waiting to offer a new glass of wine or anything else their master or new mistress might require.

When the meal came to a close, she started to say something to Cortland, but he wiped his mouth with his serviette and stood. "You will likely wish to prepare yourself. I shall see you later this evening."

He was gone before Genevieve had the chance to speak a single word.

Frustration coursed through her, but after they made love, maybe then she would finally have the chance to talk to him as they had done before. She hated this sudden formality between them and missed the teasing banter. Surely a few vows wouldn't change his entire behavior. She was determined to get to the bottom of his sudden reticence, but first she had her virginity to dispose of.

She headed for her chamber and allowed herself to be primped and primed for the duke's visit that evening. Her personal maid ensured that she was bathed and perfumed and redressed in a white, cotton nightdress, to await the arrival of her husband.

Left alone, Genevieve set her hands on her hips and spied the lone candle by the bed. It gave off only a sliver of light in the darkness. She frowned. She would have rather had the lamp turned up in order to see the duke in all his masculine glory. But maybe her grandmother was right.

With a sigh, she went over and climbed beneath the coverlet and set her arms directly at her sides and waited to be defiled.

Thirty minutes passed. An hour. Two hours.

He still hadn't appeared.

She exhaled heavily. "Where is he?" she muttered beneath her breath. She waited for fifteen more minutes and then she tossed the coverlet to the side. "This is ridiculous."

She padded to the sitting room door that separated her room from his. The fact that society was determined to keep such an antiquated system of two bedrooms for one couple had never made sense to her. It seemed that it was a perfectly disastrous way to keep that constant divide between husband and wife.

Tonight, that gap would be pushed together. If he wanted to take his time coming to her, then she would just go to him.

She padded across the sitting room on bare feet and when she reached his chamber, she put an ear to the door to listen to any sounds of movement on the other side.

There was nothing.

Curious, she pushed the door open and found the duke sitting in a chair next to the fireplace. He was fast asleep.

His feet were bare and he was wearing a purple banyan robe. The gap between his covering enticed her, because it showed off a light patch of hair on his chest. She yearned to run her fingers through the expanse, but it would sadly have to wait.

Reluctantly, she shut the door and returned to her rooms.

CHAPTER 9

The next morning when she went downstairs to breakfast, Genevieve could tell that her husband was in a foul humor. She attempted to greet him with a smile and a cheery, "Good morning," but he only gave a "Harumph" in return.

She glanced at him curiously but hoped that whatever was upsetting him would soon pass. She would like to try to tempt him to her chamber now that he was awake.

She was eager to break her fast with the fare set before her—ham and eggs, two of her favorites. But when she looked at the duke, she found that he was glaring at her darkly, rather than consuming his fare.

She swallowed her last bite rather hard, finding her appetite had diminished. She slowly set down her knife and fork and took a bracing sip of her wine, before she spoke. "Is something troubling you this morning?"

"You might say that," he snapped in return.

She tried again. "Would you care to discuss it?"

He stared at her for another minute, and then leaned back in his chair and crossed his arms. Something told Genevieve that she was about to endure some sort of lecture, because it was the same pose her father always struck when he was cross with her or one of her siblings. "You didn't come to me last night."

Her mouth fell open. "What?" Surely she'd heard incorrectly.

"Leave us!" he commanded the footmen but kept his focus solely on her. The servants scattered like leaves in the wind, but Genevieve's ire was starting to spark. "Do you care to explain yourself?"

She threw down her serviette and pushed her chair back and stood. "I will *not* sit here and be subjected to such coarse treatment from you when I waited in my room for *two hours* for you to appear. For your information, I did take it upon myself to visit you instead, but you were quite content in your chair, lost to dreamland, so I thought it best not to wake you, but to let you have your rest from the revelry you obviously enjoyed quite heartily the night before. So pardon me, *Your Grace*, for not acting like the doting wife you believed you had married. I told you a long time ago that if that is what you wanted, you had chosen the wrong lady."

Feeling as though everything had been properly said, Genevieve flounced out of the room and stomped up the stairs to her chamber. She was so angry that her blood was surely boiling in her veins. How *dare* he point fingers and accuse her of a misstep when he was the one who had failed in his duties!

She slammed her door and paced the length of her room. She couldn't sit still, she was so upset.

It wasn't until she heard the door open then slam shut again that she paused and spun around to face Cortland.

"That was an eloquent speech, Genevieve." His voice was smooth and calm, but it was his eyes, glittering dangerously, that put her mind of a cat waiting to pounce. "I'm sure you're proud of yourself for putting me in my place."

She lifted her chin. "I was merely defending my actions when you were so quick to judge me and come to such hasty conclusions that I was the one in the wrong."

"I suppose I should make amends for my behavior."

She turned her back on him. "I think the best thing you can do is leave."

"I would have to disagree. That's the last thing I should do."

She jumped, because his breath was on her neck. She hadn't heard him cross the room. She clenched her fists. "Surely you aren't eager to do something as deplorable as consummate our union now, when you've been so disgustingly proper since our vows were spoken." She sniffed. "Maybe it would be best if you sought your entertainment elsewhere—"

He grabbed her arm and spun her around, crushing her against his chest. "I'm not going anywhere. You're my wife, and if I've been *proper*, it's only because I can't think of anything else but you on my cock." When she opened her mouth, he growled, "And before you accuse me of laying with anyone, I'll have you know that I spent the entire evening at White's with the Earl of Uxbridge, before I went home—alone—and passed out in my bed almost fully dressed."

Genevieve narrowed her gaze. She wanted so desperately to believe him, but trust was the one thing that hadn't yet been fully established between them. "If that is true, then I'm relieved. But it's not as though we can do anything now. It's fully daylight."

His grinned wolfishly. "As if that would stop me from making you mine. In truth, I prefer you naked and fully visible."

Genevieve could feel herself wavering. "Do you?" she asked breathlessly.

He reached out and tore the muslin dress she was wearing directly down the middle. As it fluttered to the floor in a ruined piece of fabric, his nostrils flared. "What do you think?"

It was all the motivation Genevieve needed to give in to the powerful persuasion Cortland possessed.

She wound her arms around his neck and pressed her lips against his.

CORTLAND WAS A DYING MAN, and the only cure was Genevieve.

For so long he had denied himself a wife, a potential family, believing that history would repeat itself, but after hearing her speak so openly this morning, he was starting to believe that they could actually live together in harmony.

But first, they were going to be together as nature intended.

He yearned to pull her close, but only when they were fully undressed. He wanted to feel the slick sensation of skin on skin.

As he began to work on the fastenings of her stays, he kissed the flesh of her upper chest that was already exposed. She was soft, like the finest silk, and her scent was that of flowers and femininity all rolled into one perfect offering. He was a lucky man to have found such a woman like her. Never did he imagine it would be during one of the most erotic parties he'd ever hosted without partaking of the festivities.

When her stays came free, he saw those wonderful, taut nipples teasing him through the thin, white fabric of her chemise. He cupped each of the rounded globes and covered one with his mouth, running his tongue across the hardened tip, while he teased the other with the pad of his thumb.

"Cortland..." The breathy sigh of his name from the bottom of her throat caused him to nip the peak in approval. She stiffened slightly at first, but then her movements began to become more frenzied.

She pushed at the jacket covering his shoulders, and once he'd left her delectable body long enough to shrug out of it, she started to work on his cravat. His valet would likely cry when he knew how she had ripped it from around his neck and tossed it so casually aside, but neither did he care. His shirt quickly followed suit, until he was standing in nothing but his trousers and shoes, which he kicked off impatiently.

He lifted Genevieve in his arms and carried her over to the

bed and laid her on top of the coverlet, where he began to truly worship her. He removed the remainder of her underclothes in record time, until she was laid out before him in all her nude glory. He stood there for a moment to look his fill and then he dared to go straight for victory lane. His need to taste her overrode all else. He wanted to be surrounded by her scent, to be enveloped in it, until he didn't remember anyone else who had come before her. From this moment on, Genevieve was the only one for him.

He grasped her thighs and opened her wider to his hungry gaze. Her glistening core teased him like nothing ever before, and when he closed his eyes and licked the center of her desire, he knew he would never be the same again. It wasn't long before she was gasping, her hands clutching the coverlet on either side of her. Her hips moved in time to his movements that became more rapid with each stroke. She was getting close to her peak and he couldn't wait to be blessed with that magical moment.

When she finally burst apart, her hips stiffened and then she quivered around his mouth. He continued teasing her until he felt her relax, replete and sated.

He left her long enough to remove the rest of his clothes, and then he crawled back up her body. Her eyes were heavy lidded and a small smile graced her face. "That was… incredible."

He nuzzled the side of her neck, gently nipping the tip of her earlobe as he whispered, "We're just beginning."

∼

Genevieve's body was still humming in the aftermath of Cortland's wicked tongue. She'd long heard whispers of the "little death," but she had never understood what it had meant. Until now. She felt as though she had truly soared above her body when the first waves had struck her. Time seemed to cease entirely as pleasure filled her. It flowed through her with a delicious warmth and scrambled her entire being.

As she was floating back to reality, that's when she heard his dark promise about just beginning. She wasn't sure it was possible to even move her arm, but his growl was enough to wake up her senses. She wound her arms around his neck, and said boldly, "I want it all."

He reversed their positions until she was on top of him, her hair falling out of its confines and tumbling about her shoulders. He reached up a hand and grasped the side of her head, letting his fingers delve into the curly mass. "You're so beautiful, Genevieve," he whispered, almost reverently.

She was struck by the raw potency in his tone as she took the lead and leaned down to kiss him. Her breasts were crushed against his chest as they rolled on to their side. He touched her and caressed her until she was burning with renewed desire.

Her legs moved restlessly and she was soon crying out his name.

He slid a finger into her wet heat and started a sensual rhythm. It was a strange sensation at first, but when he added a second finger, she began to match his movements with her hips.

When he couldn't seem to take anymore, he sat on the edge of the bed and lifted her until she was straddling his lap, with a leg on either side of him. "I'll try to be as gentle as possible, but I want you so damned much right now."

His voice seemed strained as he positioned his erect cock at her entrance. She tensed for an instant as he started to push inside where his fingers had just been, but once he breached her maidenhead, she bit her lip as a burning pain replaced the pleasure.

He waited for a time, until she was used to the intrusion, and then he started to move, slowly at first, and then a bit harder and faster until the sharp pressure subsided into something more tolerable, and then into something else even more wondrous.

The slick glide of his cock thrusting into her so intimately, his dark eyes looking deeply into her eyes as he impaled her, was enough for Genevieve's ecstasy to build once again.

When she saw him bend his head and lick the tip of her breast without breaking contact with her, she found it to be too much. She clutched his shoulders, burying her head in the side of his neck, holding on as she was overcome. She bit the side of his neck, where it met his shoulder, and with a hoarse shout, she could feel it when he spent himself in her.

It was more erotic than anything she might have seen before, because it was between the two of them. *There is something fascinating about being with someone you love.*

She abruptly stilled as the truth of her words struck her. *I love him.*

But how did he feel about her?

Until she knew for certain, she intended to keep the emotions of her heart carefully concealed.

"How are you?"

She smiled at him, pushing aside any melancholy she might be feeling. "Wonderful." She touched the small set of marks on his neck. "But I'm afraid I bit down too hard."

"I loved it," he countered. "It sent me right over the edge. Pleasure and pain can ofttimes go hand in hand."

She tilted her head to the side. "How do you mean?"

He tapped the tip of her nose. "Let's not move too fast, my sweet. I have much to show you, but I don't want to scare you off too soon."

Rather than being afraid, Genevieve was intrigued, but she told herself to be patient. She might want everything that her husband had to offer, but all good things came to those who wait.

He slipped out of her and she lamented the loss, but considering she was a bit sore from their union, she decided it might be best to soak in a hot bath.

He pulled on his trousers and shirt, and then, after gathering his cravat and jacket, he went back to her and kissed her gently on the lips. "I need to run an errand to the city, but I will be back before supper this evening." Her face must have shown her disappointment, because he grinned. "Don't look so downtrodden. I don't want to be gone any more than you want me to be, but I fear there is no choice in the matter."

"Very well," Genevieve reluctantly agreed. Feeling emboldened, she laid back on the bed and propped herself on her elbow. "Don't keep me waiting overlong."

"Saucy wench." He offered a lingering look at her nude body and reluctantly turned to go. Before he left, something fell to the floor with a light *clink*.

He didn't appear to notice he'd lost anything, but as she stared at the item on the floor, a sinking sensation crawled over her as she wrapped the counterpane around her and got out of bed. "What is this?"

He paused and glanced back to see the ring in her palm. His face paled slightly as he stared at it, but then he crossed the room and took it from her, quickly setting it back in his pocket. "Nothing to concern yourself."

He bent to kiss her on the forehead, but she moved out of reach. "You're part of that ridiculous *alliance*?"

Rather than deny her claim, he clenched his jaw and admitted, "It was a club that served me well in the past."

She snorted in derision. "Yes, I'm sure it did." She spun around and put her back to him. She realized how truly naïve she'd been to believe that he could actually care for her. He had likely married her out of some misguided sense of duty to her grandfather's alliance. She'd witnessed more than one man groveling at the front door for help with one issue or another with that very ring on their hand. No doubt she was just another on a long list of grievances.

"Genevieve—"

The smooth sound of his voice did not help her raw emotions. "Please, just go."

She held her breath until she heard his heavy sigh and his footsteps retreating.

CHAPTER 10

*A*fter a restorative bath, Genevieve decided that, while the duke was gone, she would acquaint herself a bit further with her new home. She needed something to take her mind off of the latest, unsettling revelation. Engaging the assistance of the housekeeper, a pinched-faced woman with a plethora of keys on her hip and a severe expression, it didn't take long for Genevieve to earn her respect, and that of the rest of the ducal household. Since she had been raised to take on the running of an aristocratic household, she knew exactly what to do and say, most of which was authoritative in manner. She had to let them all know who was in charge when the duke was not in residence.

The first thing she did was go over the menu for what remained of the week and change whatever she thought suit her husband better. Although there was still a lot about him that she didn't know, something told her that he wouldn't care for blood pudding as much as he might a delectable shepherd's pie.

Next, she walked through every room in the manor and wrote down any changes or improvements she thought might be needed. She brought some things to the attention of the staff, most of which were problems in the guest rooms. She suggested a different arrangement and a few color schemes, and when she had their input, she planned to mention her ideas to the duke.

The last place she went was the attics. She had always hated dusty, confined spaces, but to her surprise, they were well cared for, proving that the duke employed loyal servants. Not even a place of storage like this was unkept. Again, she made a list of what might need to be discarded, including some moth-eaten clothes in a forgotten trunk, and what might be able to be reused.

She was just getting ready to change for dinner when the butler intercepted her. "There is a caller for you, Your Grace. I have taken the liberty of placing her in the parlor at present, but if I may be so bold to suggest that you keep your visit brief. She is not one that the duke would enjoy entertaining."

Genevieve's heart lodged in her throat, thinking that she might have to contend with some sort of former mistress. "Who is it?' she asked warily.

He cleared his throat. "The Dowager Duchess of Argyle."

"The duke's mother?" Genevieve's eyes widened. She had heard rumors that Argyle didn't get along well with his mother and had shipped her off to Scotland when his father had barely been cold in his grave. However, this only made her wonder what the lady had to say, and what had caused the riff between them in the first place. If she wished to make amends, the least she could do was hear the other side of the story. "Hold any tea, but I shall make myself presentable and then join her presently. The least I can do is be hospitable and prove that this is not a shunned household."

"As you wish." He bowed and took his leave without questioning her decision.

Genevieve returned to her rooms and quickly changed into something suitable for calls and for dinner that evening. Once she was attired in a light orange dress with slightly puffed sleeves and an empire waist complete with gold braiding and one of her mother's gold brooches that she had given her as a wedding present, she headed back down the stairs.

She walked into the parlor and saw a woman that might have been a duchess, if she wasn't so poorly put together. Her faded, black hair, mixed with strands of silver, might have been pulled up into an elegant chignon at some point, but now, it hung down in a pitiful mess. Even her clothes were rumpled and dusty as if she had slept in them for days. She was sitting in a chair, but one of her legs was propped over the side in an entirely unladylike fashion. But her blue eyes were sharp when they lit on Genevieve.

The smile she offered wasn't warm or motherly, but rather cynical in nature. "You look too innocent to be Cortland's bride."

Genevieve wasn't sure whether to take that as an insult or a compliment. Instead of sitting across from the lady, she remained standing and smoothly turned the conversation back on her. "You don't look very much like a dowager duchess."

She shrugged. "After living in the wilds of Scotland for the past several years, I suppose I have adopted some of their barbarian ways." She sighed heavily. "I used to be gorgeous. Every man in London and beyond wanted me."

She chose to ignore the latter comment, and instead, addressed the concern about Scotland. "I haven't known them to be anything but kind," she noted.

Her reply was a snort. "Then you haven't been properly schooled." She sat up straighter. "Allow me to be blunt."

Genevieve wasn't sure she could be any other way.

"The stipend that my son has granted me isn't enough to keep up with the lifestyle that I should have had in my advanced years. I need him to double it."

"I'm sure whatever my husband offered has been very generous—"

"Are you daft, girl?" She interrupted crossly. "Didn't you hear what I just said? I demand more!"

Genevieve was starting to understand why Cortland was reluctant to see his mother. Something had obviously upset her mind. She saw the butler appear out of the corner of her vision, but she held out a hand to him, indicating that he should not intervene. "It is not my decision to make. You will have to speak the matter over with the duke when he returns."

"Worthless gel!" The dowager shouted. "Haven't you spread your legs for him yet? If you do it properly, he'll lay the world at your feet."

Genevieve had to admit she had a way with words when it came to being crass and uncouth. "If you don't wish to talk to the duke, then it appears we have nothing further to discuss and I must ask you to leave."

She walked over to the parlor entrance expectantly.

The lady sniffed in a haughty manner, before she stood. "You will regret this."

She stomped out of the room and slammed the front door on her departure.

∽

CORTLAND HADN'T BEEN ENTIRELY truthful with his wife. But then, he hadn't wanted to spoil the surprise.

He'd gone to London that morning, that much was true, but it wasn't for business purposes. At least, what he might have led her to believe. Instead, he had gone there to pick up the belated wedding gift that he'd commissioned for her. He'd received word just that morning that it was ready, when he had hoped it might have been done before they'd left London. But at least he had it in his possession now, and he hoped this was a step in the right direction to winning her love. He no longer had any doubt in his mind that he was head over heels in love with her. She had made his life whole, when he hadn't realized he needed more. But from the instant he'd spied her at his house party, the first word that had crossed his mind wasn't an obscenity, or some word that might show his annoyance otherwise.

Mine.

He'd wanted her out of that house as quickly as possible, because he hadn't wanted to take the chance her head might have been turned by another. From that very first meeting, he was infatuated, even though it had taken him a while to understand why she might be different from the other females of his acquaintance. It was because she wasn't anything like those women. She was the furthest sort from his mother that he could possibly imagine, and that alone made her worthy.

He still might not know Genevieve's favorite color, but he knew she would be loyal to a fault. She was someone who would stand up for what she wanted without backing down. The rest of it would surely follow. After all, they had a lifetime to talk about their likes and dislikes. But tonight, she would know how he felt about her without reservation.

Cortland wasn't the type to believe in love at first sight, but it hadn't taken more than a second glance before his heart had become engaged.

He rode his mount up the drive to the estate but paused when he saw a lady stalking down the front steps and getting into a hired carriage. His entire body stiffened, because he knew who it was. His mother had dared to step foot on this land again when things had become too difficult for her, or so she claimed. She was hardly left to rot in the wilds of Scotland as she liked to bandy about to whomever would listen. She liked to play the victim at the hands of her ruthless son who gave her a pittance to live on, when in truth, it was a very generous allowance.

He kept his horse in the middle of the path, forcing the carriage to stop. He ordered the driver to remain where he was, and his authoritative voice must have been convincing, because he bobbed his head respectfully.

He maneuvered his horse around the side of the carriage so

that he could peer inside. As suspected, his mother was inside. She didn't appear to notice they had stopped moving, because she was muttering to herself, but then she shouted out the window, "Driver! I didn't order you to stop—" Her command abruptly ceased when she saw him. "Cortland, my dear. There you are."

"Stop with the theatrics, Mother. Why are you here? To try to get more money from me? It won't happen," he said flatly.

Her eyes started to fill with tears, a tactic she had tried many times to gain his sympathies. What she didn't realize was that she'd done it so many times to his father that it didn't faze him anymore. "You don't understand. I'm sick. Would you throw me to the wolves, instead of offering me comfort in my last days?"

He snorted. "What sort of illness is it you purportedly have this time?" Again, it wasn't a new claim that he hadn't heard before.

Instead of replying to his question, her lower lip trembled. "Do you still hate me so, Cortland? I'm your mother! I gave you life!"

"I don't hate you. I simply don't care about you."

She leaned closer to the window and offered a whisper that could be heard across the country. "I have syphilis. The doctors have confirmed it. Before long, it shall affect me with open wounds that will not heal, blindness, and eventually death. I merely want to feel at ease when I pass on. Can you not grant me that much mercy? Or are you that cold hearted?"

Cortland warred within himself. He had the feeling that, for the first time in her life, she was actually telling the truth. "I will consider it. That is all I can promise at this time."

He kicked his horse in the flank, causing it to continue moving forward.

"I love you, my boy!"

He ignored the call behind him, because he knew it wasn't true. It was *never* true. She was a charlatan who preyed on his emotions to gain what she wanted. It hadn't changed since the time he was a child, and it hadn't changed now.

GENEVIEVE TOOK one look at Cortland and she knew he must have had an altercation with his mother. She had never saw anyone look as though they could commit murder—until now. Although she was still upset about finding the WD ring, she pushed that aside for now.

"Cortland?"

He pinned her with a dark glare. "What did she say to you?"

She was taken aback by his open hostility. She had never known her husband to look as though he could strike out at her, but she also knew that he wouldn't act on the impulse. She took a deep breath. "She demanded her allowance to be doubled and said I should regret it if I didn't convince you to do so. I told her she would have to speak with you." She decided not to anger him further by their full conversation. In truth, she would rather have forgotten that conversation had even occurred.

Some of the stiffness eased from his shoulders, but his frown was still present. "I need a drink," he grumbled, and then headed for the library.

Genevieve followed at a more sedate pace. She could tell his mother was a sore subject with him, but something told her that speaking about her was the only way he might be able to heal and move past his wounds.

She gently shut the door behind them. It would be best if the servants didn't overhear their conversation, because hopefully, it would cause her husband to speak more openly.

"Cortland?" she spoke gently, and slowly moved closer to him, but not to the point she would anger him even further. She had to be delicate, like soothing a spooked horse.

He had his back to her, but she heard the decanter as he set it down firmly on the sideboard. "I have despised that woman as long as I can remember."

Genevieve kept her hands clasped before her and waited patiently for him to continue. If he spoke, at least it was better than keeping all of his hurt and frustration bottled up inside.

"She made a cuckhold out of my father. It would have been bad enough if she'd been discreet, but she chose to parade her numerous lovers in front of him." He paused, and she could see his hand tighten on the glass tumbler. "She is the reason he died. The strain was more than he could bear. The part that I found unforgiveable was that she didn't shed a tear at his funeral. Standing at the gravesite, she looked as though she was bored with the entire ceremony. I know my father wasn't cruel to her. He never raised his voice, nor his hand. She had no reason to treat him as she did, and yet, my father still doted on her, giving her anything that she asked for. She nearly bankrupted the estate with her extravagant lifestyle. She took numerous trips to the continent, and even though it was obvious she was enjoying her life to the fullest, she still drained everything that my father had —his money, his devotion, and even his love—to support her amusement." He released a heavy breath. "I *hate* her because of what she did."

Genevieve's heart went out to him, not in pity, but in empathy. She felt sorrow that he hadn't been able to have the sort of loving family that she'd grown up with. There was no doubt in her mind that her parents loved one another and continued to do so.

Perhaps if she told him that he wasn't alone anymore, he would be able to let go of that strong emotion. "I know she hurt you, and I'm sorry for it."

He snorted and downed the remaining liquid in his glass.

"I hope you know our marriage won't be like that, because I love you."

She knew she'd said the wrong thing because he suddenly

CHAPTER 11

A rawness swept over Cortland; he was a man with a bruised heart. When his mother told him that she was dying, he had been inclined to deny her claim. But what if she spoke the truth for once? Although he had cast her to the wilds of Scotland, he wasn't sure how he would feel if she wasn't actually on this earth any longer.

His gut was tormenting him with a twisting sensation, so he wanted a way to forget, if just for a while, but then his wife had followed him into the library, where he'd foolishly poured out his misgivings like some sort of child that was looking to be consoled.

He wanted to demand that she leave him, but before he got the chance, she was slipping her dress off her shoulders. "You need proof that I love you?" she challenged softly, as she began to fully disrobe in front of him. "How about the fact I trusted you enough to marry you? I gave up my freedom and my innocence to someone I barely knew. Now that I know you are part of the alliance, my confidence has faltered, but my devotion to you continues to remain steadfast. In my heart, something told me that I was making the right decision."

When her chemise pooled around her feet on the floor, leaving her unclothed, except for her stockings and slippers, she slipped out of the material at her feet and started to walk toward him. He was captivated by the gentle sway of her hips and the light movement of her breasts. He clenched his fists at his sides, eager to take her into his arms and love her thoroughly. But how did he know she wasn't another charlatan like his mother? A female who wanted to control him and use him for what she could gain?

When she reached out a hand to touch him, he closed his eyes, as his cock sprang to full attention.

"I want you, Cortland. Say that you want me too."

He couldn't stop himself. He opened his eyes and reached out and crushed her to him, his hands roaming over her back then down to cup her buttocks. "You drive me mad with wanting you," he said harshly. He reached between them and freed himself and then lifted her into his arms, impaling her straight on his eager cock.

She threw her arms around him and kissed him with abandon. He held her tight, not wanting anything to separate them. Finally, when they were breathless, he buried his head between her breasts, and laved one pert nipple and then the other. Her head fell back on a moan, and Cortland couldn't take any more. He carried her over to the settee where he switched positions and kept her on his lap. He gritted his teeth as he grabbed her hips and started a sensual rhythm of thrust and retreat. Her breasts swayed and teased him until his body tightened in preparation for his release.

Just as he was about to be overcome, he realized what he was doing. This was his wife, Genevieve, and he was treating her as some common whore, rather than with the respect and attention that he should be showing her. He was acting just like his mother, without any care to her—only himself.

He cursed and moved her off of him. Her eyes were dazed,

confused and hurt with his sudden withdrawal. His cock was just as upset, but he shoved the stiff member back inside his trousers with a shaking hand. "Forgive me," he muttered, and then he left the room without any further explanation.

FOR THE DAYS FOLLOWING, Genevieve didn't know where her husband was. She was told later that day that he'd left, but he hadn't found it necessary to tell her where he was going, or when —or perhaps *if*—he would be back. She wasn't sure what had caused him to leave her so abruptly in the library, but until she understood his reasons, there was nothing she could do but wait.

Tears were her companion in the interim, and she was grateful that he wasn't there to see her red-rimmed eyes, knowing that he was the reason for her upset. But perhaps he wouldn't care. Anytime she thought of that possibility, she burst into another round of self-pitying waterworks. She thought that the start of her courses might have had something to do with her emotional upset, but she had cried more in recent days than she ever had in her entire life.

Love truly could be a wicked thing.

She finally found some solace in the gardens, where she spent most of her afternoons in contemplative solitude. She wasn't sure how she might act when the duke returned. She doubted that she would fall into his arms in gratitude, but neither did she wish to continue this heart wrenching separation. She prayed that whatever he was doing, it was something for the greater good and that he hadn't already tired of her.

She sat on the stone bench surrounded by an array of daisies and held a single white bloom in her palm. She considered plucking the delicate petals from the stem, like she had as a child, but she was afraid that it would end poorly.

But just because she had nothing else to occupy her time, she started to pluck them away from the yellow center. "He loves me. He loves me not." Each time one of them fluttered to the ground, a tear began to fall in its place. Her fingers began to shake and with each pass around the flower, she started to lose hope that anything might change between her and the duke. She'd confessed her feelings to him, and he'd more or less cast them aside.

"He loves me not," she whispered.

"He loves you."

She spun around to see Cortland standing a short distance away from her. She quickly stood and lifted a hand to dry her cheeks that were stained with the evidence of moisture.

He remained where he was, perhaps because he was unsure of his reception. Genevieve should be furious, unable to stand the sight of him, but the heart was a fickle thing, making her yearn to be held in his arms again. He looked like he had ridden to hell and back. He was still wearing his greatcoat, and it was splattered with mud from his journey. His expression looked weary and ragged, as if he had done a lot of soul searching.

"I was a fool to leave you like I did." His throat worked and he cast his gaze to the ground, before he lifted his eyes once more. "I don't know that you'll ever forgive me, but I hope someday you might be able to do so."

The only thing she wanted was the answer to the question that had been bothering her more than anything else. "Why did you go?"

"I needed to find out if what my mother had claimed was true. She told me that she has syphilis. I traveled to Scotland and spoke to her doctors and discovered it was."

A surge of relief pulsed through Genevieve. "Why didn't you just tell me that?"

"Because when I left, I wasn't sure where I was going." He shoved a hand though his hair. "I didn't know if I needed absolution from a priest or to be shackled in the streets. All I know is that I'd hurt you and I hated myself for it. I hated that I never told you about the alliance, but that I was treating you like a common trollop even more."

Genevieve swallowed hard over the lump in her throat.

"When I discovered that my mother was actually being sincere, I did as she asked. Not that I raise her stipend, but that she would be settled somewhere comfortable for what remains of her days and receives the care that she deserves. I took her to London to the Lock Hospital under an assumed name. She begged me not to tell anyone who she really was, and I agreed, but I was careful to make it known she should have the best care." He paused, as if finally thinking back on everything that had transpired. "At the end, I found that I could not desert her in her time of need, because I am better than that." His dark gaze pierced her. "But that is only because of you. I wouldn't have thought twice about tossing her out on her ear any other time, but you have made me into a better man, when I used to focus on being bitter."

Genevieve started to tremble, and she had to turn away to keep from flying across the expanse and into his arms, begging for his love.

When she felt the slight pressure of his hands on her arms, she started to tremble.

"I realized I didn't need the alliance anymore, so I submitted my resignation to your grandfather. *You* are all I need." His hands tightened slightly. "Please say you still love me after everything I put you through. I can't go back and reclaim any of my actions. All I can offer you is a fresh start."

He gently turned her back to face him. And then he got down on one knee. He withdrew a small box from his pocket and opened it to reveal the most beautiful diamond ring she had ever seen. "My darling, Genevieve. You have the opal ring that belonged to countless Duchesses of Argyle, but I want us to start a new tradition. To have a fresh start with a clean slate." He took her hand and slid it on her ring finger next to the heirloom ring. "If you will accept my hand again, I promise that my heart is fully attached to it. I never wish to leave your side for the rest of my days. And I hope that they are well numbered for both of us."

Genevieve couldn't hold back any longer. She fell to her knees and put a hand on either side of his face. "You might be a maddening duke at times, but you're also my *perfect* duke. I wholeheartedly accept your proposal." She kissed him lightly. "I love you."

"And I, you." He ran a gentle finger down the side of her cheek. "Let's go inside where I can love you properly."

She smiled. "I would like that very much, Your Grace."

AUTHOR'S NOTE

A stag party, that I mention before the wedding, is similar to an American bachelor party. These parties have been around since ancient Greece—the last night for a gentleman to enjoy a night of feasting and revelry before entering into the marital state. A hen do is the female equivalent to the bachelorette party, but since rules were a lot more strict for women in history, I decided that Lady Genevieve might enjoy a quiet evening at home, learning how to be a proper wife.

I'm sure many of us have played the plucking flower game – he loves me, he loves me not. Did you know that this is French in origin? I found several mentions of this game in the Victorian era, but the earliest notation I found was from an 1820 illustration from the Goethe novel, *Faust*, aptly entitled, *The Decision of the Flower*. So it might have been introduced formally a little later than when my story takes place, but I like to think perhaps not.

The Lock Hospital was a real place in London. It was used specifically to treat venereal diseases, and although most of the aristocracy would have recovered at home, no matter what their illness, considering the previous discord in the past between my hero and his mother, I thought it best that she willingly admit

AUTHOR'S NOTE

herself under an assumed name, with her son as her acting benefactor.

Last, but not least, is the Erotic-o-rama. I wanted to come up with something entirely silly and I bet that when we've all had a bit too much to drink, it's possible. And since the words erotic and panorama were around at the time, I thought I would take another slight liberty.

AFTERWORD

I'd like to thank you for purchasing this book. I know you could have chosen any number of stories to read, but you picked this one and for that I am humbled and grateful! I hope that the romance captured your heart and added a smile to your day. If so, it would be awesome if you could share this book with your friends and family and post a review! Your feedback and support will help improve my writing and help me to continue growing as an author.

ABOUT THE AUTHOR

Tabetha Waite began her writing journey at a young age. At nine years old, she was crafting stories of all kinds on an old Underwood typewriter. She started reading romance in high school and immediately fell in love with the genre. She gained her first publishing contract with Etopia Press and released her debut novel in July of 2016 - "Why the Earl is After the Girl," the first book in her Ways of Love historical romance series. Since then, she has become a hybrid author of more than forty titles, published with both Soul Mate and Radish Fiction, upcoming works with Wolf Publishing and Dragonblade, as well as transitioning into Indie publishing. She has won several awards for her books.

She is a small town, Missouri girl who continues to make her home in the Midwest with her husband and two wonderful daughters. When she's not writing novels filled with adventure and heart, she is either reading, or searching the local antique mall or flea market for the latest interesting find. You can find her on most any social media site, and she encourages fans of her work to join her mailing list for updates.

https://authortabethawaite.wix.com/romance

Made in the USA
Monee, IL
31 August 2023